You bring such joy to my life — Dad

BACON GREASE

& Baseball

John S. Viccellio

ISBN 978-1-54397-444-7 eBook 978-1-54397-445-4

Dedicated to the memory of my wonderful grandmothers, **Inez Deahl Showalter** and **Annie Blair Hardy.**

Special thanks to Harvey Cohen, Lucy Beam Hoffman and Elizabeth Olney for their support, assistance, and encouragement.

Contents

Contents

The Invitation

Mama and Daddy spent weeks trying to convince me it would be a wonderful experience for me to spend the summer with Gramby because…"it would be good for you to get away from the same old summer city stuff"…and "there is so much to do there"…and "Gramby has a big woods in the back and a creek"…and "Gramby always thought you were the smartest"…and "she needs the company"…and "you will really have fun"…and "it isn't good for Gramby to be living alone"…and "there are Gramby's buttermilk biscuits"…and "her chicken and dumplings"… and "you will love her brown sugar pie"…and….

When we got in the car, I was sure I was in for a long boring summer of 1948 in Gramby's little town of Coldbrook, Virginia. Let me tell you what happened.

Coldbrook Field

S tanding in Gramby's side garden, I watched a hawk circling overhead searching for an early lunch. It soared in looping circles, catching an updraft, letting out an occasional sharp screech, and flapping its wings to keep going. Its elegance and stamina captured me. I arrived at Gramby's just the day before and was trying to find something fun to do.

Two boys about my age came riding up and stopped their bikes at the edge of the garden. The older looking one said, "You must be the grandson. Your grandma told my Mom how you would be here for the summer and how we are to look out for you. What's your name?"

"I'm Charlie. Where do you live?"

"We're the Haymore brothers. I'm Thad and this is my little baby brother Stubby." Thad was tall and lean, and I could see why his not so little brother was called Stubby. "We live on my Dad's farm just down the road. Do you play baseball?"

"Yes" I answered, but I didn't mention that I was new at it. "I brought my new glove... and my bike."

"Swell," Stubby said. "We play on our farm and are trying to get some teams together in town. Do you want to play?"

"Sure."

And that answer changed my life.

For that summer…and for the rest of my life…baseball became a passion.

When it wasn't raining, I rode my bike to Thad and Stubby's farm, and we played ball in their cow pasture. Their cousin Bart, Junior Parker who lived up the street from Gramby, and Barry Lee Jamison often joined us from the next farm. Barry Lee wasn't much of a ball player, but he liked being part of the crowd. He was the only one who didn't mind going after a ball that rolled down the hill to Stony Creek.

We played five or six man baseball using rocks for bases, honesty for foul lines, and a chicken wire backstop Mr. Haymore built. That backstop wasn't big enough to stop a wild pitch, but it helped make the cow pasture feel like a ball field. We spent hours shagging flies, trying to field grounders despite the uneven surface, and working on our pitching. Sometimes Thad's two little sisters hung around and chased foul balls for us.

There was a large briar patch at the edge of the pasture, a tangle of wild berry bushes and sharp thorny plants. It had a magnetic attraction for baseballs. We didn't have a lot of "spare balls;" we needed all we had. If a ball were hit in that direction, we hollered like Br'er Rabbit, "Please, don't throw me in the briar patch." When one went in, it took time and delicate maneuvering to remove it. It was my first experience with thorns, and it didn't take long to learn to be super careful around them. A long-handled hoe was the instrument of choice. Despite the caution, we often had to call on Thad's Mom to clean up a bloody scratch with Mercurochrome. Later in the summer we ate ripe blackberries right off the bushes, at least when hungry birds left a few.

When it got too hot, we moved to the Haymore backyard in the shade of big oaks and tried to develop a curve ball. We worked all summer trying to throw a curve; not one of us was successful. If it were too hot even in the shade, we went down the hill and jumped in Stony Creek to cool off.

Thad and Stubby took me to town to see "Coldbrook Field" and meet the other boys who played there. Coldbrook Field was a vacant lot by the railroad. It was dusty with red clay, full of weeds, and by the end of June had baked hard. I think it was especially sculptured to create bad hops. In that summer I contributed a good bit of skin, spit, and sweat to its composition. We had no grass, no coach, no uniforms, no trophies, no refreshments (other than the Mason jar of water Gramby made me take), no team photos, and...best of all...no parents. It was *real* baseball...an official Major League baseball and genuine wooden Louisville Slugger bats. Everyone wore his hat with the bill in front, on and off the field. We kept our fingers in our gloves.

When the boys realized I had a new glove, they all had a theory on how to break it in. A baseball glove is produced now with a readymade pocket; you can take it from the box and use it the same day. In those days you had to break in the glove and make your own pocket. The boys insisted that I needed to rub it down with neatsfoot oil, and I spent hours that summer oiling my glove. I tied it around an old ball with strips of an inner tube at night to make a pocket and pounded my fist into it constantly. I went through four bottles of neatsfoot oil in less than two months and had the toughest knuckles in Coldbrook.

It's strange what you recall about boys with whom you played decades ago. I can't remember the names or anything remarkable about some of them, but others stay firmly in my memory.

Andy was the catcher. He could stop a hard one in the dirt...at least most of the time. He had a strong arm and could throw the ball to second without a bounce. He sometimes threw it to centerfield without a bounce.

Phillip had a speech impediment; he lisped and stuttered. At first I thought he was plain stupid, but I learned how bright he was. He had great hand-eye coordination; he could hit!

Jimbo was the youngest in a family with six older sisters. He was used to getting his way and was one of the last ones chosen when we divided up. He liked to tell everyone on his side what to do and how to play. When we were short of players (we were almost always missing a right fielder),

Jimbo's sister Sarah was allowed to play. Actually, she was better and faster than most of the boys, and that did not make Jimbo happy at all. Sarah put two fingers in her mouth and whistled louder than any of us. She did it often to call attention to her hits. As much as I tried, I could never whistle like that; what I got was a "whoosh."

Matt was the bravest boy on the team and the only one who kept his head down and eyes on the ball to dig one out of the dirt. He was the obvious choice to play first base and usually the first chosen.

Tommy was the fastest kid on the field, but he had trouble catching the ball. He dropped at least half a dozen balls in any afternoon, but he was great on the base paths.

Harley always complained. Nobody ever threw him a strike, and nobody ever got him out.

Lance must have had a runny nose the entire summer. He had a special way of using the sleeve of his shirt to wipe his nose, and everyone teased him about his grungy shirt. His real name was Lancelot. When he struck out or dropped a ball, something that happened often, his full name came out. "Hit the ball, Lancelot." "Catch the ball, Lancelot."

There were five boys named John. Over time they came up with unique nicknames for each one and so I met Johnny, Jackie, Johnson, J.B. and Shorty. Shorty insisted on playing shortstop; "It goes with the name," he said. When a freight train passed the field, Shorty liked to stop play and count the cars in a loud voice. The rest of us would holler, "Play ball," or some unrepeatable epithets, but Shorty just kept counting. Finally, the others joined in counting, and then one or two called out-of-order numbers until it confused everyone. Shorty gave up, and the game resumed.

When Sarah came to the ball field, her best friends, Nancy Shorter and Chickie Frye, usually accompanied her. They heckled us unmercifully. They celebrated our mistakes. At first, it upset me when they drew attention when I dropped a fly. Thad said, "Don't let those stupid girls bother you. We ignore them." It was good advice.

6

We all had our favorite teams and players. Gramby's paper had full write-ups of each Major League ball game. This was before baseball expansion and the one sentence newspaper summaries we get today. I ran to get the paper each morning to read the sports section. It started a habit I follow to this day. Occasionally a headline in another section of the paper caught my eye, and I learned something interesting about another part of the world. I looked into Gramby's collection of *National Geographic* magazines which I found fascinating.

Baseball made me a reader.

The daily baseball articles included detailed box scores. I asked Gramby for a notebook and recorded the stats of my favorite player and figured out how to determine his batting average. In a few weeks I also figured out...on my own...how to calculate earned run average.

Baseball gave me a reason for math.

When I got interested in baseball records, Gramby bought me a baseball annual at Gravely's Drugstore. It opened the idea of history for me. What year did WWI end? 1918, the year before the Black Sox scandal. What year did Lindbergh fly the Atlantic? 1927, the year Babe Ruth hit 60 home runs. What year did WWII begin? 1939, the year Ted Williams came to the Red Sox.

Baseball turned me into a history buff.

I came home one afternoon, went to the cookie tin in the kitchen as usual, and said to Gramby, "We had quite a group show up for baseball today."

"What was so special?"

"Well, we almost had the twelve disciples playing."

"Twelve disciples? What do you mean?"

I counted them off. "There was Jamie Curry and Jimbo, the five Johns, Thad, Phillip, Matt, Tommy, Bart, Andy, and Simon Parker. Phillip brought a new kid named Pete who came for the first time. We only missed Judas;

I guess nobody in Coldbrook wanted to name a son Judas. Jimbo's sister Sarah figured it out and told us we were such a holy group, we couldn't use bad language on the ball field."

"That sounds like wise advice. I'm glad to see that Sarah has been paying attention in Sunday School."

"It didn't last long. I think Jimbo sounded off just to make Sarah mad."

The day before I left Gramby's, the boys organized a farewell game at Coldbrook Field to say goodbye. I don't remember who won, but I do remember that it was a grand afternoon. I dropped an easy fly (my new glove wasn't completely broken in yet), and Tommy stole two bases in the same inning. Lance wore a clean shirt. Sarah hit an "infield" home run (three errors after her squiggler to third base which Jimbo threw over Matt's head). Thad claimed that she hit a curve ball he left hanging over the plate. Shorty let a train pass without counting. He said he did it in my honor.

Gramby, Aunt Bell, and Judge Law came to the game along with several other adults, and there was a lot of cheering from the spectators. Gramby brought a wash tub iced down with RC Colas and a big box of blackstrap cookies.

Every kid should have a Gramby like that.

I didn't return to Gramby's the next summer, and I lost track of those boys. Years later Thad and Stubby met me in front of the Coldbrook Baptist Church after Gramby's funeral. I didn't recognize them at first, but, when they told me who they were, we hugged and tried to catch up on over forty years in a few moments there in front of the church. "How's your curve ball?" Stubby said. He didn't have to tell me he was thinking about baseball at Coldbrook Field, shagging flies in his Dad's cow pasture, and skinny dipping in Stony Creek.

2

Bacon Grease

Mama always described me as a "fussy eater." The foods I disliked far outweighed the number of things I ate. Even at my age, my tastes had become narrow and rigidly defined. Most of what I disliked were things I had never even tasted. They "smelled funny," or they "looked different." I did not want to try anything new. My summer in Gramby's kitchen, however, changed all that. Her secret was bacon grease.

Gramby cooked bacon every morning for breakfast: eggs and bacon, pancakes and bacon, waffles and bacon, grits and bacon, buttermilk biscuits and bacon. I loved bacon; still do. She had a pot on top of the stove into which she poured the bacon drippings; bacon grease was always available. Only a few things she cooked were without at least a spoon or two of bacon grease. She transformed bland, tasteless vegetables into delicious treats with the magic of bacon grease. French fries were tastier, and chicken was crispier.

She had a special Gramby way of getting me to try new things.

I never ate black-eyed peas before my summer in Coldbrook. Gramby came home one day with a half bushel of black-eyed peas. "Why don't we learn how to shell peas today." It wasn't a question.

She showed me how to squeeze open the end of the pod and run my thumb down the rest of the shell and push the peas into a bowl. Little did I realize that my just learned black-eyed peas technique worked as well for green peas, butter beans, lima beans, and brown peas (the ones without the black eyes).

"Let's look for any bad ones. They will either be rock hard or white. If you see any, we'll discard them."

She heated water in a pan and, when it started boiling, she put in a dollop of bacon grease. "I always add bacon grease to make them better." Then she put in a cup of my freshly shelled black-eyed peas.

At dinner that night she served the black-eyed peas I helped prepare. I ignored them for a while, but she said with a smile, "Why don't we try our peas now. Try some vinegar on them." I felt an obligation to take at least one bite.

I liked them. I finished them and asked for more.

Gramby then offered variations. She served black-eyed peas with chopped onions. Wonderful! She served them with crumpled bacon. Delicious! She served them with onions or scallions and bacon. Fantastic! I was hooked on black-eyed peas.

One evening the black-eyed peas were on the plate next to rice. In the course of eating, the two were mixed. What happened by accident became one of my favorites: peas and rice. I found that mixing with rice was also a tasty way to eat green peas, brown peas and butter beans.

The next vegetables that Gramby introduced were green beans. She called them "snap beans," and I soon understood why. She also called them "string beans," and I soon understood that too. She showed me how to snap off the end of the bean, leave it attached to the string that ran down the edge, pull the string to the end, and then snap it off. That required skill which took me a few times to gain. She then snapped the beans into several pieces, put them in a skillet, and cooked them with bacon grease.

I can't say I ever liked them, even with the bacon grease. All too often a string was left on and was caught in my teeth. I had the same problem with snow peas. Even though I can now buy stringless beans and snow peas, I want to snap off the ends and look for the strings. I still don't feel comfortable eating them.

Gramby introduced me to new foods by getting me to help in their preparation. I peeled apples to make apple cobbler, apple sauce and apple butter, and we canned apples to make pies over the winter. I crushed grapes and berries to make jams. We canned peaches, tomatoes, cucumbers, snap beans, beets, butter beans and corn. We pickled watermelon rind and cucumbers.

One day after lunch she said, "Why don't we make blackstrap cookies."

"Why are they called blackstrap?"

"Because I make them with blackstrap molasses."

"I've never heard of blackstrap molasses. Is it good?"

"It's strong tasting. Not many people like it right out of the bottle, but it adds a great taste in certain recipes. My grandma gave me this recipe, and I think you will say the cookies are delicious. Wait and see."

Gramby put the ingredients in a bowl and asked me to mix them. When she was about to add the molasses, she said, "Why don't we try a taste."

"I'll try, but just a little; you said I might not like it."

She put a bit in a spoon, and I tasted it. She was right; I didn't think I would ever want to taste such strong stuff again. It didn't even taste sweet, and I thought molasses was supposed to be sweet.

She added the molasses to the ingredients; we mixed it together, made balls of the batter to place on a cookie sheet, and put them in the oven. When the cookies came out and cooled for a few minutes, she said, "Why don't we try one."

I did, and they were delicious. Blackstrap cookies went on my "gotta have" list. Gramby kept making them for me. The cookie tin in the kitchen was never empty.

She made wonderful mashed potatoes; bacon grease was the magic ingredient. We peeled and cut potatoes into about half-inch cubes. She then fried them in bacon grease until they were cooked on the inside and crisp outside. She put them in a bowl and mashed them with a potato masher. She handed me the masher and let me finish the job. She added cream and melted butter and mixed everything with a big metal whisk. What she created was creamy and buttery but with a crunch from the crispy fried parts. Often she served it with a topping of chopped chives or the old standby: crumbled bacon. I've seen no one make mashed potatoes the way Gramby did, and I've never tasted any so good.

We put a dozen hard-boiled eggs in a big jar filled with vinegar and some pepper corns. "I'll put in some beet juice to add color. Meemie Payne taught me how to pickle eggs," she said. "You can take them anywhere without refrigeration." I took them to baseball and to the movies on Saturday. The other boys tried some and asked me to bring more.

Gramby's chicken and dumplings were magical; they were so good I asked for them almost every day. I think her secret was in the dumplings. She used her buttermilk biscuit recipe for making the dumplings. She let me squeeze out small balls from the dough and drop them into hot thick gravy and chicken pieces cooking on the stove.

She introduced me to beef and pork meatloaf with mushrooms, onions and sausage bits mixed in. She let me grind the meat. Stuff the meat in the top of the grinder, turn the crank, and out comes ground meat. It was fun. She covered it with bacon and baked it in the oven. It was perfect with her mashed potatoes.

And then there was her brown sugar pie, unquestionably the most wonderful, delicious, and fantastic pie I ever ate. It is my favorite to this day.

One day when we had finished lunch in the kitchen Gramby asked me, "Have you ever had peanut butter candy?"

"No, but you know how much I like peanut butter."

"Well, why don't we make some. I'll show you how; it's easy."

She mixed butter and powdered sugar with something she called vanilla extract to make a white dough. She then rolled it out on a sheet of wax paper and covered it with peanut butter. Using the wax paper, she carefully rolled it into a log. "We'll put this in the refrigerator until it gets hard; it's too soft to cut now."

After about an hour she took out the log and cut it into quarter inch rounds. "Why don't we try some."

We did, and I added another item to my top twenty list.

A few days later Gramby was frosting a devil's food cake with chocolate butter cream icing. We had icing left over, and I said, "I have an idea. Why don't we put some of that chocolate icing on the peanut butter candy?"

We did, and I discovered the wonderful combination of chocolate and peanut butter.

How grateful I am that someone else also made that discovery. How grateful I am for Reece's Peanut Butter Cups!

3

The Woods and the Creek

I loved spending time roaming around Gramby's woods and by the creek. So much was new. She often walked with me and pointed out the different trees and bushes in the woods; she seemed to know the names of them all and tried to teach them to me. After a few of our walks, I was comfortable identifying oaks and maples and dogwoods, which were fairly easy, but the shrubs were too many and too much alike. I already knew what a pine tree looked like. I learned to recognize the differences between the mosses and ferns and lichens and mushrooms in her woods.

I also heard an important lesson. "In *this* family," she said, "we do not eat wild mushrooms."

There were two huge stones in her garden, both of which were long, rounded and smooth. They were so big and unlike anything else in the garden I couldn't imagine how they got there. Gramby said they were there when she moved in, and she just built the garden around them. They were great places to sit and think and plan and dream about playing Major League baseball. If only I could master that curve ball.

Those stones were big enough that I could lie down on them. I watched the buzzards and the hawks circling overhead during the day and shooting stars and the Milky Way at night. I saw John Wayne in *They Were Expendable*, a movie about PT boats in the war, and saw myself at the helm, commanding one of those fast, powerful fighting ships right there in the garden. One of those stones was my PT boat, and in my imagination my torpedo always sunk the bad guys.

Is that why I joined the Navy?

I didn't realize at first that the creek in back of Gramby's woods was Stony Creek, the same one that ran below Thad and Stubby's farm. I made a number of discovery journeys, sloshing up and down the creek from our woods until I was under the bridge on the main road out of town and came to the edge of their farm.

There is much for a city boy to learn from a creek.

A tangle of trees, bushes and vines marked the edge. In deeper wider parts the water hardly seemed to move. When it narrowed, it rushed. Stones…lots of stones in Stony Creek…formed mini dams that caused the water to jump and tumble. It gurgled; it whispered. When the creek turned, the outside edge was deeper, and the water flowed faster. The inside edge was shallower and likely to have deposits of sand and pebbles. There were quiet spots where the water was barely moving; they were homes for tadpoles and minnows.

Gramby helped me make a cheesecloth and coat hanger net. I used it to catch minnows. Piling rocks in a narrow area directed the water to run into my net. I did indeed catch minnows, but nothing much larger than a finger. I put them in a Mason jar but soon realized they didn't stay alive for long. Gramby explained that minnows need oxygen just like we do. "They get it from the water, and when it's used up in a Mason jar, they die."

I used one of Gramby's magnifying glasses to take a closer look at those minnows. I saw a rainbow of colors that were barely visible without the glass. Light reflected off the scales on their bodies. I cut one of them open to see what was inside. The inside things were so small that, even with the magnifying glass, I couldn't recognize anything but its intestines.

Was I becoming a scientist?

Stony Creek was full of trash. People upstream were certainly careless about throwing stuff in the creek. I started carrying a bag with me into which I put the trash I collected. I was amazed to see what was washing down the creek: bottles, cans, kitchen scraps, empty cigarette packs, chicken necks and feet, black-eyed pea pods, bones, all sorts of paper items, chewing gum and candy wrappers, snap bean strings, building materials, and more. Much of it was lodged between rocks or caught in the tangle of vegetation along the edge of the creek. I even recognized what I thought was dog poop and deer poop.

Was the water drinkable? It was clear enough I could see the minnows flitting about. I filled a Mason jar with creek water and, shaking it around, saw it was full of fine debris. I didn't know if the water contained just tiny dirt particles or what else might be in there. It would have been nice to have had a microscope to discover what was there, but I had already seen enough poop in the creek to know for sure I didn't want to drink any of that water. How did the minnows and tadpoles deal with all that gunk?

I talked with Thad and Stubby about taking on a project to clean up Stony Creek from Gramby's woods to their farm, and we agreed to do it. We enlisted Bart and Barry Lee Jamison to help; the five of us spent hours up and down the creek filling up buckets of debris. Thad's dad hauled if off for us in his pickup. We asked the boys at the ball field to help, but they said it was our creek and we could clean it up. They left it to us, and frankly I think we did a creditable job. Thad and Stubby's parents and Gramby told us how proud of us they were for doing such good work on that creek.

Birds filled Gramby's woods and garden. At most times of the day we could hear birds singing and calling. She told me the names of many of the birds whose calls she knew…wrens, chickadees, cardinals and sparrows. When we walked around together, she pointed out the different birds.

A bird made a call in one part of the garden and another answered. "Those are wrens," she said.

"How do you know what they are?"

"I've seen them so many times when they make that call, so I recognize it now. A wren is one of the loudest birds in the garden…so small but with such a big voice."

"What do you think they are saying to each other?"

"Probably something like 'Stop on your way to the nest and pick up a few extra bugs. The kids are getting hungry again.'"

I kept a notebook, and over the summer I was able to identify what I called "color birds:" cardinals, goldfinches, blue jays and black crows. I already knew robins and buzzards and hawks. In time I added wrens, chickadees, nuthatches, tufted titmice, various finches and sparrows, and several types of woodpeckers. It was my introduction to ornithology and gave me an enduring interest in birds. Gramby bought me a bird book and helped me learn how to use it to identify new birds.

Every kid should have a Gramby like that.

I kept that bird book and notebook going for many years, recording bird sightings wherever I went.

Her garden and woods were alive with animals. Gramby called them "critters." It's safe to say she didn't find many of them welcome. Deer ate her roses and other flowers. Raccoons made a mess of the trash cans as they scrounged for food. Squirrels and possums dug up her flower beds. An army of rabbits feasted on almost anything in their reach that was green.

Another group of creatures in the woods and garden were insects. Except for the butterflies and honey bees, I would only call the rest "pests." Honey bees and spiders didn't worry me although I never liked walking into a spider web. Leave them alone and they ignore you. I learned to give a wide berth to wasps and yellow jackets. They like their space and react vigorously when humans intervene. When they sting, it hurts. Lesson learned.

I was sitting on Gramby's back steps watching a pair of robins searching for worms. I glanced away and noticed there was a horde of caterpillars eating Gramby's potted plants. I ran in to tell her. "They're green with yellow stripes and they're stripping the leaves right down to the stems."

She just laughed and said, "I've been waiting for them to show up. Those caterpillars are fattening up so they can become Black Swallowtail butterflies. They eat my parsley plants every year about this time; I plant extras for them. They love parsley."

She explained the life cycle of butterflies: from a butterfly egg comes a caterpillar which grows and attaches itself to a safe place, spins a cocoon to protect itself, and emerges a few weeks later as a beautiful butterfly. "Many insects go through the same cycle,"

A few weeks later we began to see Black Swallowtail butterflies flitting around the flowers in Gramby's garden. They especially seem to gather around her roses. Gramby said, "Now you see why I planted that extra parsley."

It was my first lesson in entomology.

There were legions of gnats whose sole goal in life was to find their way into my ears and nose. Several times they got into an eye, very irritating, and Gramby had to flush them out. Flies were a constant nuisance, particularly if I were eating a lunch time sandwich on one of those big stones.

The top of the pest list...or should that be at the bottom...was reserved for mosquitos, ticks and chiggers. I knew about mosquitos; we had them at home. Gramby stayed on the lookout to overturn standing water; "That's where the mosquitoes breed," she said. Their bites itched and only got worse when you scratched. Understand that this was before the age of insect repellents. Someone told Gramby that peppermint was a good deterrent. I tried to rub leaves from Gramby's mint patch on my arms and neck and face. I still got bites.

Ticks and chiggers were new menaces in my life. It was easy to pick up a tick when walking through the woods. Brush against a bush and a tick comes off on your socks, pants or shirt and seeks a spot on your skin to suck your blood. Gramby had me stand for a tick inspection every night. I stripped down to my undershorts, and she checked me all over for ticks, with special emphasis on my head. When she found one, and she found them frequently, she used a pair of tweezers to pull them off...gently.

"You can check your private parts yourself," she said. "It's important that we find ticks; their bites can make you sick with an infection."

Chiggers are the worst. They are red, spiderlike, and move incredibly fast for such tiny creatures. They are difficult to see because they are so small, particularly hard to see on colored material. You don't know they are there until they dig in. They like to find a nice spot on your skin, tunnel in. and start feasting on your blood supply. The area reddens and itches... terribly. Gramby said the only way to deal with them is to smother them. She brought out a dab of bacon grease to cover them. The sites continued to itch painfully for weeks, some for months.

Of all the things that happened at Gramby's that summer, the itching of the chigger bites is impossible to forget. I hate those little red critters!

When I started going frequently to the woods and creek, Gramby suggested that I wear dungarees and my brogans to protect myself from the critters found there. She warned me especially about copperheads.

"They're the only snakes around here that are poisonous. We have others...black snakes and little green garter snakes...but the copperheads are the ones you have to worry about. You will most likely see them around the creek, but they can show up anywhere."

"What do they look like? How can I know? What if I see one?"

She described its appearance and showed me a picture. I studied that picture and dreamed about it at night. I decided if it weren't black or green, I was going to run away.

I did see copperheads on several occasions. The only scary time was when I kicked a pile of dead leaves in the woods, and there was a copperhead. I didn't need the picture to make sure. There it was, a few feet away from me with raised head. I backed off very slowly, very, very carefully.

I saw black snakes and green garter snakes frequently about Gramby's garden. I wasn't afraid of them, but I kept my distance.

I had a dream that summer that hundreds of snakes were in the electric and telephone lines in front of Gramby's house. There were snakes of all sizes and colors, climbing the telephone poles, entangled in the wires, climbing over each other, hanging down, turning their heads back and forth, hissing, spitting out their tongues…at me. All the while I was watching, directly below them, unable to move, trembling, waiting for them to fall down on me.

That dream was many decades ago. I have had tens of thousands of dreams in my life, almost all of which I don't remember at all. Why, of all those dreams, do I remember that one so vividly after all this time? I close my eyes, and I can see it once again…the telephone poles, the snakes, and me…trembling still.

4

The Silver

It started with a napkin.

The first night I was at Gramby's, we sat down to dinner. She read a verse from the Bible and offered a brief prayer. She included a few words about me and said she was grateful that I had come. She prayed we would have a good time together over the summer.

She said, "Why don't we put our napkins in our laps."

"Why?"

She smiled and said, "In *this* family we put our napkins in our laps."

I put the napkin in my lap.

She had to suggest we put our napkins in our laps only a few times after that.

I saw the wisdom of this family tradition a few days later when I dribbled a big blob of catsup from my hamburger onto my lap...right on the napkin. A look of discovery must have painted my face. I looked up; Gramby just nodded, smiled, and handed me another napkin.

It never occurred to me that I was about to undergo a summer of dinner table training. I had not signed up for that, and Mama had said nothing about it. I'm not sure Gramby had such a plan in mind when I came, but she saw the need for it and took advantage of our meal times to change forever the way I eat.

The next lesson began when Gramby said, "Why don't we set the table for dinner."

"Sure," I said, and put two plates in a stack on the table, and forks, knives, and spoons in a pile next to the plates. Gramby was quiet for a few moments, smiled, and said, "Why don't we learn to set the table properly. In *this* family..." she started, and I knew another family tradition was coming. I learned family traditions always came with a Gramby smile.

She then showed me what was "proper:" a table mat for each plate, napkin folded on the left of the plate and the silver in its place. "Silver" was Gramby's term for all tableware regardless of its content. Her pattern for placing the silver was a dinner fork left of the plate and a salad fork on the outside. On the right is the knife, blade facing in, with the spoon on the outside. She then placed a salad plate and glass on a coaster in their "proper" locations.

Gramby went to the sideboard and picked up a pair of small glass containers and tiny spoons and placed them on the table with a pepper shaker.

"What are those?"

"They are salt cellars. In *this* family we have always used salt cellars instead of salt shakers. This way you know exactly how much salt you are putting on your food. I will show you how to use the little spoons."

"What about dessert plates?" Again she smiled and said, "Dessert plates and forks go on the sideboard. We will get them when we clear the table. There, see?" she said, pointing to the set table.

"Sure."

"Next time I'll let you do it, now that you know how."

I learned that "in *this* family" there was also a "proper" way to hold the silver when eating and cutting. I arrived at Gramby's holding a fork in my fist and thought that was a comfortable way to shovel food directly from plate to mouth in one easy, effort saving motion. "Why don't we hold our forks like this," she said, and showed me how she held her fork just so with her thumb on top and the fork resting on her finger. I presumed that is how we do it "in *this* family." After a few trial runs with Gramby's coaching and encouragement, I learned yet another family tradition. Then she showed me how to cut out a bite with the side of the fork.

I was grateful to hear that in *this* family we don't have a different tradition for holding a spoon.

There was one marvelous exception. In *this* family we may eat fried chicken with our fingers; using either one or both hands is acceptable. The only additional requirement is the frequent use of the napkin to keep the mouth and hands clean and keep them from contaminating the silver used for the rest of the meal...and my pants.

Using the knife and fork to cut things the way we do it "in *this* family" introduced me to another family tradition. Normally I stabbed the meat or vegetable with a fork in my fist and cut it into pieces all at the same time. My first lesson was on a slice of Smithfield ham, and Gramby introduced me to an altogether complicated ritual.

One: transfer the fork from the right to the left hand.

Two: place fork face down on the ham with forefinger on top of the fork

Three: put just enough pressure on the fork with the forefinger to hold the ham steady

Four: with the forefinger on top of the knife, slice off a small bite-size piece of ham

(Rule: In *this* family we only cut one piece at a time)

Five: place the knife on the edge of the plate

(Rule: In *this* family once a knife is used, it is never put back on the table. This rule applies to all pieces of silver)

Six: return the fork from the left hand to the right hand

(see above for "proper" holding of the fork)

Seven: place left hand in lap

Eight: slide the tines of the fork under the piece of ham

(Rule: In *this* family we do NOT use our fingers to push things onto a fork; bread or a roll or the knife (last resort) can be used to coax the ham onto the fork)

Nine: raise the ham with the fork and place the ham in the mouth to eat

Ten: place the fork on the plate with the handle on the rim while eating

(Rule: In *this* family we do not talk while chewing)

Eleven: repeat the process for each bite of ham as necessary until the last piece is eaten

(Rule: In *this* family we eat all our ham)

Twelve: wipe hands and mouth with the napkin when finished

(Rule: In *this* family we do not wipe our hands on our trousers or sleeve)

I took several weeks to master the knife and fork ritual, but I finally did and remember feeling proud of myself. I must admit that I have never conquered the temptation to cut more than one bite at a time. I still feel guilty when I do.

I learned in later years she taught me the "American" way of handling silver. The European method seems much simpler, but I never felt comfortable eating that way. I confess that I have seen European friends trying to balance peas on the back of a fork. It made me appreciate the way we do it in *this* family.

After dinner we cleared away the dishes, and Gramby said, "Why don't we do the dishes together. I'll wash and you dry." Here was yet another family tradition that included my learning that everything has a proper place.

Gramby introduced me to more family traditions. "In *this* family we take our hats off at the table." "In *this* family we don't put our elbows on the table." "In *this* family we wash our hands before eating." "In *this* family we place our silver neatly on the plate (handles on the edge, all to the center) when we have finished eating." "In *this* family we fold our napkins and put them on the table when we are finished." "In *this* family we seat our guests first before we sit down."

I could not have imagined there were so many traditions associated with eating. Before my summer with Gramby, I paid no attention to how people eat. I have since been a keen observer of others and cannot help but compare them with the way we do it in *this* family. Why, there are even people out there who don't follow the knife and fork ritual.

After a few weeks I set the table to her exact specifications, used my silver in the proper way, executed the knife and fork ritual flawlessly, and kept my napkin in my lap and my elbows off the table. Gramby said she was delighted to see what a polite young man I was. "In *this* family," she said, "when someone does something special, we celebrate. Why don't we drive up to Gravely's Drugstore and have a banana split."

Every kid should have a Gramby like that.

5

Gravely's Drugstore

In Coldbrook there were three places where you could see almost everyone in town.

Of the two food markets, Mr. Toler's New Food Emporium was the most popular by a ten to one margin among the locals. I liked the New Food Emporium because Mr. Toler had a world class selection of candy. I think Gramby saw an opportunity to bribe me into having a good time spending the summer with her; she never failed to give me a nickel for candy when we stopped at the New Food Emporium. We usually went uptown to the grocer several times a week, so I remained well supplied with candy over the summer. I liked the hard stuff, and, at a penny a piece, Mr. Toler had barrels of it: red, green, blue, yellow, orange, cubes, balls, squares, all to entice a boy loaded with money in his pockets.

Mr. Toler raised chickens, and a freshly killed and dressed "frying size" chicken for dinner was only a phone call away. Several of them found their way regularly into Gramby's chicken and dumplings. Mr. Toler also prepared his own sausage.

The second important place in town was the Coldbrook United States Post Office. Mr. Willard delivered mail to our house six days a week, but Gramby always found a reason to stop by the Post Office, to buy stamps or pre-stamped postcards, or to mail or pick up a package. She sent post cards as thank-you notes to everyone who had done something nice for her. She told me, "In *this* family we send thank-you notes," and she encouraged me to begin a practice I still try to follow.

I soon realized that what she wanted at the Post Office was to get the latest town gossip from Mr. Waterson, the Postmaster. Sydney Waterson and his wife Agnes were longtime friends of Gramby and my grandfather Lane Loudermilk Payne, and he was a very willing source of the town news. Gramby described him once as "a man who keeps his ears open."

For a while I stood around and shuffled my feet while Gramby and Mr. Waterson talked. Then I discovered the WANTED posters.

I read each one and marveled at the evil deeds done by those men. Some of their crimes I had never even heard of. I had to ask Mr. Waterson what "postal fraud" meant. I remembered their names and crimes though. Whenever we returned to the Post Office, I immediately went to the WANTED posters to find out the status of those terrible people. When I was about to ride my bike uptown to play baseball, I began to ask, "Gramby, do you need anything at the Post Office today?" I wanted the latest information. Surely those crooks should have been caught by now.

It made me wonder about the Coldbrook police. Didn't they know about those bad men running around loose? Their pictures were right there on the wall at the Post Office. I would have recognized them anywhere. Why didn't they do something? I looked carefully at men I saw on the street, particularly those who looked like they were trying to hide something. What would I do if I saw one of the men on the posters? At night, alone in my room, I imagined all sorts of bad things about those men as I was trying to go to sleep. Could they be in our town? In Coldbrook? Right now? In our neighborhood, just waiting to break one of Gramby's windows and steal something? What was that strange noise I heard outside in back of the house?

During the whole summer I never saw a single WANTED poster removed, only additions.

My favorite place in town was Gravely's Drugstore. It served Coldbrook as the primary local source for both prescriptions and a host of patent medicines. Pharmacist "Doc Gravely," as he liked to be called, learned his trade during his stint in the Army Medical Corps in World War I and came home and opened a drugstore. He learned enough in the Army to pass the state exam and get a license when he returned. He also learned how to concoct his own special brand of "Gravely's Tonic." When taken internally, it was "guaranteed to ease back pain, settle the stomach, and cure the common cold." Gramby said she knew people who would swear by it. "I tried it once," she said, "but it made me dizzy."

There were several families in town named Gravely, and all of them pronounced it in two syllables with the "a" to sound like the "a" in "fat." Doc Gravely pronounced it in three syllables and the "a" to rhyme with "fate," even though most of the Gravelys in town were cousins or otherwise related to him at some level. Gramby made a special point on my first visit to introduce me to Doc Gravely and said, "This is Charles Hester Payne, the new man in my life." And then she turned and said, "Now be sure to pronounce his name correctly; it's GRAY-vuh-lee."

Later I asked, "What difference does it make?" Gramby said, "It makes a heap of difference to Doc GRAY-vuh-lee." She said Mr. Waterson told her several of the Gravely cousins some time back had accused Doc Gravely of putting on airs. Doc Gravely said he didn't mind; it was good for business. It was his practice to wear a long white coat when he was in the drugstore. Gramby said, "He tries to look like a doctor; Doc Gravely likes to make a good impression on his customers. I believe he thinks it adds credibility to his tonic."

He gave an area of the drugstore over to a large display of "Gravely's Tonic," three convenient sizes and in cartons of six bottles. A sign was always there that read, "Special Prices. Today Only!" with "Adults Only" in small letters. Next to the display were the newspaper and magazine racks.

If Gramby...and Doc Gravely...had let me, I would have spent hours there going through the magazines. I saw it as my personal library.

Gravely's Drugstore was the only place in Coldbrook that sold comic books and *The Sporting News*. It was there that I followed the adventures of the greatest heroes in the world. I could read about Superman, Batman and Robin, the Green Hornet, the Shadow, Wonder Woman, and Captain Marvel. I marveled at how lame newspaper boy Billy Batson could be transformed into the mighty Captain Marvel by shouting, "SHAZAM!" I learned what SHAZAM stood for:

S for Solomon for wisdom
H for Hercules for strength
A for Atlas for stamina
Z for Zeus for power
A for Achilles for courage, and
M for Mercury for speed.

My Uncle Walter drove a Mercury, and now I knew why he drove so fast. I had heard of Solomon in Sunday School, and I thought Atlas had something to do with a skinny man on the beach getting sand kicked in his face. I didn't know who those other heroes were, but I could understand how Captain Marvel always won his battles. A boy could build his life around those characteristics.

I tried to sneak into the drugstore unnoticed and sit on the floor next to the comics, out of sight of Doc Gravely behind the prescription counter. I read as many of the comics as I could before Doc Gravely inevitably came out into the store and spied me on the floor. "Up or out," he said. "Pay up or get out." I thought it was not a very nice way to treat a potential customer. I did avoid him enough to keep up with my heroes over the summer without having to pay for too many comics.

The Sporting News was another matter. That newspaper has changed a great deal in the intervening years (it is now digital only) adding coverage of other sports. In those days it was almost exclusively devoted to baseball, and it was in baseball I had my deepest interest. Each weekly issue of the paper was full of information. It covered every Major League team with an extensive article. Player profiles helped me learn about their records and their history. It was all a real baseball fan needed, but there was too much information to read in snatches on the floor of Gravely's Drugstore each week.

Thad and Stubby showed me I could pick up pop bottles on the side of the road and turn them in at the New Food Emporium for a few pennies each. There were a lot of careless people throwing valuable bottles out of car windows. When I had saved up enough money, I spent it on *The Sporting News*. Gramby must have noticed my commitment to save to buy the newspaper instead of candy, and one day she said, "Why don't we buy *The Sporting News* each week. I can see how much you like it."

Every kid should have a Gramby like that.

The prime attraction at Gravely's Drugstore was the soda fountain. It covered one side of the building and had six stools with bright red leather covers. They sold anything a person could want at Doc Gravely's soda fountain: ice cream sodas, sundaes, milk shakes, malts, phosphates, lime-ade and lemonade ("freshly squeezed right before your eyes"), and floats.

I could not believe my eyes when I saw Gramby order my first banana split. It had a sliced banana, scoops of chocolate, vanilla and strawberry ice cream, lathered in real whipped cream, and topped with three maraschino cherries. I loved that banana split, but my absolute favorite item was a float of RC Cola and a double scoop of vanilla ice cream.

Popular specialties at the soda fountain were oatmeal-raisin cookies, freshly baked each day by Mrs. Gravely. She brought them into the drugstore late each morning while they were still warm for the lunch crowd. You smelled them as soon as you walked into the drugstore; they were usually sold out by the end of the lunch hour.

Doc Gravely's soda fountain was the most popular spot in town, and it was usually crowded, particularly with teenagers. My baseball friend Harley's older brother Hector was the soda jerk, and "jerk" was the perfect title. He didn't seem to care much for us younger patrons; his attention was always on the older kids, especially the girls. He took forever to fix my float, tried to short change me and my friends, and talked down to us. "Get off those stools and let the real customers have a seat." It is remarkable how quickly young boys can become keen mathematicians when paying with their own money and getting change. When Doc Gravely came around, Hector right away put on a different face, full of smiles and thank you's, and "Please, what can I do for you, young man?" I understood where Harley got the attitude he displayed on the ball field--too much time being Hector's little brother.

Doc Gravely, without knowing it, played a key role in getting me into big trouble with Gramby. Shorty's father had a deal with Doc Gravely to let Shorty pick up cigarettes for him. He worked the night shift at the mill in the next town, was a heavy smoker, and spent most of the daytime hours in bed. Shorty brought the money for the cigarettes to the drugstore and asked Doc Gravely for his dad's order. Doc Gravely then went through the routine of going in the back room to "search for the order." He returned with the cigarettes in a bag, money was exchanged, and no one was the wiser. I suppose Doc Gravely knew he shouldn't have been giving Shorty his father's cigarettes, but Doc Gravely was famous for doing what he could to keep his important customers happy. Shorty's father was a regular purchaser of Gravely's Tonic.

At first Shorty's father had to call Doc Gravely and tell him he was sending Shorty for cigarettes. In time the phone calls became infrequent and then stopped, but the routine continued anytime Shorty showed up with the money.

Hector observed Shorty's visits over time and finally saw him accidentally drop the bag and a pack of Camels fall out. Hector told Harley, Harley told Jimbo, and the two boys hatched a plot that would involve all of us at the ball field.

Jimbo made sure his sister Sarah wasn't there when he announced the plan. It was simple; each boy would contribute a few pennies and Shorty would get us a pack of Camels at Gravely's Drugstore. Then we would go into the old shed at the edge of the ball field where no one could see us and light up. Doc Gravely would think it was a normal purchase for Shorty's father, and no one would know the difference.

Everyone but Shorty thought it was a great plan. It took two weeks of intense pressure before he finally gave in. By then Sarah was in on the secret and surprised everyone by jumping in as a willing conspirator; she was the first to put in her pennies. She even volunteered to take the small change to the New Food Emporium to get a single quarter. "Shorty's father would never send twenty-five pennies to Doc Gravely for cigarettes," she explained.

The next debate was over the date. Everyone wanted to execute the plan right away, but Shorty kept putting it off. He finally agreed that he would add the pack to one of his father's orders.

The plot went off without a hint of suspicion from Doc Gravely. Shorty timed his visit to the drugstore on Hector's day off. Nobody trusted Hector to keep his mouth shut.

When Shorty arrived at the ball field, he gave thumbs up and we all cheered. We immediately headed for the shed and fourteen kids jammed in. Shorty handed the pack to Jimbo, who obviously relished his role as leader of the plot. He handed out the cigarettes. Matt and J.B. backed out but hung around to watch. Matt said something to the effect that his Dad would kill him if he found out. They wanted their money back but got twelve "no" votes. We then discovered that nobody had thought about matches, and everyone screamed at Jimbo for this rather important oversight.

Sarah spoke up and said she would go to the New Food Emporium and make an excuse to get a pack of matches. She came back, and we lit up.

The small shed became heavy with smoke, full of coughing and sputtering. There was so much smoke, my eyes were watering. Someone suggested we get out of the shed, but Jimbo said we couldn't because someone might see us and our parents would find out and we'd all be beaten backside.

I had never smoked a cigarette, but I tried to act like a veteran. I didn't even know how to hold one. I tried to take a drag without inhaling, just letting the smoke out of my mouth. I didn't mean to inhale, but I finally did and immediately felt a sensation going through my entire body. It scared me because I didn't know what was happening. Lance got sick, ran outside and threw up. Sarah said she was dizzy but liked it and would do it again.

The smoke session was over quickly. Not one of us suggested a second.

Thad, Stubby, Junior and I rode our bikes home and swore on the Bible that we would never tell on each other.

When I walked into the house, trying to be quiet, I went straight up to my room, put down my baseball gear, and went to the bathroom and brushed my teeth. I didn't want Gramby to smell my breath. When I came down, Gramby asked me, "What have you been doing?"

Why would a Gramby ask such an innocent question? When a boy comes in the house and doesn't yell, "Gramby, I'm home." When a boy doesn't drop his baseball gear in the entry hall like he always does. When a boy doesn't go straight for the kitchen to the refrigerator or the cookie tin. When a boy doesn't give Gramby a hug when he comes home. When a boy doesn't make eye contact. Could there be a reason?

I answered casually, "Nothing."

A boy will learn over a long period of growing up that he will hear "What have you been doing?" from parents, teachers, coaches, bosses, and the worst possible answer in every case is "nothing." "Nothing" always means "I've done something...something really bad or really stupid...that I don't want you to know about." In the court of family justice "nothing" is an immediate admission of guilt; now we just have to find out what the crime was. Let the probing begin.

I learned there is another dangerous question: "Where have you been?" And an equally wrong answer: "Nowhere."

Gramby was quiet for several minutes and then said, "Have you and your baseball friends been smoking?"

How could she possibly know? So fast? Who squealed?

"Who told you?" Another wrong response, another clear admission of quilt.

"You did."

I was dumbfounded. I had said nothing. I looked at her, unable to speak.

"You did," she repeated. "You smell to high heaven with tobacco smoke. It's in your clothes and in your hair."

Caught, I confessed. The only things I left out were the roles of Shorty and Doc Gravely.

Gramby gave me the smoking lecture, short version. Then she asked me to promise not to do it again.

I promised.

Gramby said she wouldn't ask me to tell on the other kids, although she could guess which ones were involved. And in one of the greatest acts of grace in my young life, she said, "If you keep your promise, I don't think it will be necessary to tell your Mama and Daddy."

Every kid should have a Gramby like that.

6

Aunt Bell

Gramby had three sisters. Probably her closest friend was her sister Mary Bell. By the time I came along, everyone in the family called her "Aunt Bell." She was only eleven months younger than Gramby, and they grew up together almost as twins. Gramby certainly loved Aunt Sarah and Aunt Caroline, but I think Aunt Bell was her favorite.

She lived in Coldbrook and ran the Hotel Grover. It wasn't what I thought a hotel would look like, but that's what Aunt Bell called it. It was a large three-story building in the center of town next to the post office. She rented individual rooms (two baths on each floor at the end of the hall) and several apartments with bath and kitchen. Gramby's good friend, Miss Pat, rented an apartment there, and there were several other longtime residents. Judge Law and Nadine Pruitt had become like members of the family.

Aunt Bell had an apartment on the first floor next to a spacious entry room. She called it her lobby. For us in my generation, she was a loving, caring, fun great aunt. Each one of us was convinced we were her favorite. I am sure I was. She smothered us with hugs. She showered us with attention. Aunt Bell loved us.

I got to know her so much better when I came to Coldbrook for the summer. The first time Gramby and I visited her she welcomed me with a gigantic hug and immediately offered me one of her peanut butter cookies. Those cookies became a major incentive to drop by the Hotel Grover when I was uptown. She became a big part of our life together. Aunt Bell even performed the knife and fork ritual as we do it in *this* family; I did notice that she frequently cut more than one forkful at a time. She always had a tin of cookies on her kitchen counter, and she said, after the welcoming hug, "Why don't we have one of my peanut butter cookies."

The Hotel Grover gave Aunt Bell enough income to keep her going. She loved to go to auctions around the county, looking for a good deal, and furnished her rooms with antiques. She was partial to solid wood...cherry, walnut, and mahogany, especially mahogany. When there was no space in her rooms for more antiques, she filled up her basement with the overflow. She was quick to offer them to any and all newlywed nieces and nephews to help start their households. A prized possession is a solid mahogany chest that years later she gave me and my new bride.

Aunt Bell talked in superlatives and exaggerations. Everything or everybody she referred to was always the richest, biggest, largest, meanest, highest, lowest, nicest whatever in the county. She tried to attend every funeral in the area. She was constantly after Gramby to go with her. The dear departed may have been a stranger but was connected, however remotely, to someone in her life.

I stopped by one afternoon after baseball, and I was eating a cookie in her kitchen. We were talking about when I would be going home and back to school. She wasn't acting like herself, far too quiet. She acted like her mind was somewhere else. She just let me talk. I was surprised when a man stumbled into the kitchen. His hair was hanging down in his face; he looked like he hadn't shaved in several weeks; his clothes were dirty and wrinkled. I could smell his foul breath even across the kitchen. He looked like one of the hobos we saw sometimes by the railroad tracks next to Coldbrook Field. He walked unsteadily, and I thought he was going to fall. He caught himself with a quick move of his leg and then rocked back and forth. He took another step and again almost fell. He grabbed the back of a chair to catch himself.

Aunt Bell said, "Davis, this is Charles Payne, Elizabeth's grandson, who is spending the summer with her. Charles, this is Davis Grover."

I stood and reached out to shake his hand. "Nice to meet you, sir."

He held on to the chair, just stared at me, and continued rocking. His only acknowledgement was to let out a grunt.

I felt uncomfortable, didn't know what to say or do. I decided that I needed to get out of there right away. I made an excuse and headed for the lobby. Aunt Bell followed me to the door, put her arm around me, and said, "I'm sorry you had to see him like that."

I left and thought, "*So that was Uncle Davis Grover.*"

When I got home, I told Gramby about meeting Uncle Davis, and how he looked, and how sad Aunt Bell was."

"I will call her. It must be hard for her."

"I don't understand what was going on there. Why was he there? Why was she so upset?"

"Let me try to explain; I think you are old enough to understand. This is a sad story."

She told me about Aunt Bell and Uncle Davis.

Aunt Bell met Davis Grover when she came to Coldbrook to help Gramby after my Dad was born. She married Uncle Davis the night before he shipped out to France in WWI to fight the Germans. Most folks thought she was lucky to have caught the handsome young carpenter who inherited a tobacco farm near the river south of Coldbrook. It had prime bottom land. Gramby said her mother and Papa were certainly pleased. Uncle Davis left her pregnant, and Aunt Bell was overjoyed. The thrill was short lived, however, when she lost the baby after several months. The complications left her so that she was never able to have children.

Uncle Davis, as he was now called in the family, returned to a hero's welcome in Coldbrook. Gramby said it was never clear what Uncle Davis had done in France to be proclaimed a hero, but at least Aunt Bell was glad to have him safely home. A number of men from Coldbrook and the surrounding county did not make it back in one piece, or at all.

The euphoria left forever when she saw that Uncle Davis had come home from France with a drinking problem. Uncle Davis turned his attention to alcohol. Aunt Bell turned her love and attention to her family, particularly her nieces and nephews.

Uncle Davis returned to the family tobacco farm. It was rundown from lack of oversight while he was away, but Aunt Bell told Gramby they were excited about the challenge to start their new life together and make a success of the farm. After that, Aunt Bell never volunteered much about the farm except to respond that everything was "getting better." Gramby said she noticed that, when she visited Aunt Bell, Uncle Davis was almost never there. Aunt Bell explained that he was off on a carpentry job to help bring in a little extra money and would be back in time to pull tobacco.

On a late summer afternoon, Gramby said she arrived to find Aunt Bell sitting by her kitchen table, sobbing. "I don't know if I can take any more of this," she said through her tears. "He just wired me to send money to get him out of jail up in Culpepper. He's in for public drunkenness." She then confessed she was too ashamed to admit that Uncle Davis was always half drunk or worse, neglected the farm, came and went without warning, called her collect for money to bail him out of some predicament... or get his tools out of hock...or get him out of jail. He was mean to her when he eventually showed up at the farm...usually sick, drunk, and broke. The worst part was that he placed blame on her and berated her for losing their baby.

"But he's so sweet to me when he's sober," she cried.

For several years Aunt Bell lived through a recurring cycle of Uncle Davis' drunkenness, leaving, sending for money, returning, sobering up, leaving, and getting drunk again. She finally persuaded Uncle Davis to sell the farm. They sold that farm at a perfect time. It was just before the crash of '29 and the depression, so they got top dollar. Then, after the crash, she had the money to buy the hotel at a rock bottom price.

Uncle Davis continued to make her life a misery.

Aunt Bell told Gramby she had decided that her life had to be her own to live. A lawyer in Coldbrook worked out a separation agreement, which Uncle Davis accepted. Unfortunately, the misery for Aunt Bell didn't end with the agreement. Uncle Davis wasn't out of her life at all. He continued to arrive without warning, sick and drunk, pester and beg her for money, spend it on whiskey, and then leave, only to return some days or weeks later. Gramby only found out later that Aunt Bell continued to give money to Uncle Davis and care for him when he showed up, even after the separation.

"Why?" I asked. "Why did she let him come back and make her life so miserable?"

Gramby said Aunt Bell simply couldn't stop.

Several weeks after she told me about Aunt Bell and Uncle Davis, I answered the telephone to a sobbing Aunt Bell. "I need to talk to Elizabeth."

I called Gramby to the phone. I heard her say, "Oh, no." and another "No. Oh, Bell, what can I do? We'll be right there."

When we got in the car, she said, "Bell just got a telegram." She was silent for a minute. "Davis is dead." More silence. "They are sending the body by train."

"What happened? How did he die?"

She didn't answer immediately. "He killed himself outside the jail in Macon. He apparently shot himself."

"Why would he do that?"

"Davis was a sick man. Alcohol. He got to the point that he couldn't stop drinking. We don't know what happened to him in France or what he saw or experienced. He wouldn't talk about it. Whatever it was changed him. Ever since he came home, it's been a problem. It's almost ruined Bell."

"He must have been drunk when I saw him at the hotel."

"Yes, he was. Bell called me after you were there to tell me about it. She was embarrassed and sorry that you had to see him in that condition."

The week of Uncle Davis' funeral was crazy. Gramby and I spent several days either making things to eat or passing out food in Aunt Bell's lobby. She arranged with the Ashley Funeral Home to bring the body to the hotel for viewing in a small room off the lobby.

They did a good job on Uncle Davis. His hair was cut, his face was shaven, and he was in clean clothes.

It was the first time in my life that I saw a dead body. I didn't stand around and look at him very long. I thought it was creepy.

It was also my first funeral.

I imagined that a funeral would be a solemn service that lasted maybe an hour or so. But that was not the case in Coldbrook.

Uncle Davis' funeral and all that went with it lasted for a good three days. For everyone except Aunt Bell and the family it was a major social event. Town folks dressed up in their Sunday finest to call on Aunt Bell, view Uncle Davis' corpse, and offer a few words of consolation. Doc Gravely even took off his white coat for the occasion and came in a suit and tie. For two days before the day of the funeral the lobby at the Hotel Grover was full of people. It was a time of feasting as everyone who came brought something to eat…"so the family wouldn't go hungry." Judge Law and Nadine Pruitt stood by at the food tables to receive and distribute the food. They let me help.

People came with tuna salad, chicken salad, pimento cheese, and cucumber sandwiches, all cut into triangles (without the crust). They brought ham biscuits, assorted cheeses and crackers, bowls of pecans and walnuts (shelled), cookies, brownies, cakes and pies. They brought candy dishes, watermelon rind pickles, and fresh vegetables cut into bite-sized pieces. I counted at least seven different styles of deviled eggs. I tried them all. Mr. Toler's New Food Emporium sent a large platter of fried chicken each day, and Mrs. Gravely brought her famous oatmeal-raisin cookies. There were sausage balls and Vienna sausages wrapped in dough.

Twice we ran out of toothpicks and napkins, and they sent me to Mr. Toler's to replenish.

Most people in Coldbrook did not know Uncle Davis personally; many had heard of him and his actions around town and knew that he was Aunt Bell's husband. Consequently, they didn't quite know what to say to Aunt Bell. A few talked about his military service in WWI and how brave he must have been, but most of their comments were aimed at Aunt Bell and her sorrow.

Every time someone said something nice to her, she would get teary eyed. Gramby and I stood close by her as the well-wishers paraded through. She had a few stock responses, only changing a word or two.

"I am glad/pleased/moved/touched/grateful/appreciative that you have come."

"You are so nice/thoughtful/helpful/generous/special/kind."

People were quiet with solemn faces when they were in line to speak to her. I noticed that as soon as they said their consoling words, most of them headed for the food table and loaded up. There followed happy greetings, animated conversations, and even laughter could be heard from time to time.

The funeral itself was not much to remember. The preacher had never met Uncle Davis, so he didn't have a lot to say about him. He did make a point about his service to his country and spent the rest of his talk on repentance and forgiveness. Maybe he knew more about Uncle Davis than I realized.

It was nice to see family members...Aunt Caroline and Aunt Sarah, aunts and uncles and cousins, and Mama and Daddy and my sisters. I didn't tell them much about what I was doing with Gramby in Coldbrook, only that it was okay.

A week after Uncle Davis' funeral, Gramby and I drove Aunt Bell to the cemetery. We gathered fresh flowers from Gramby's garden to place on the grave. As we stood there, Gramby put her arm around Aunt Bell.

She was quiet for a long time. "I prayed so long that he would find peace, but I didn't want it to be in this grave."

Aunt Bell continued to live in the Hotel Grover well into her 90s. A week before she died, I was in Coldbrook and drove her for what would be her last visit to Uncle Davis' grave. She stood there, leaning on me, and, with a tear rolling down her cheek, she said quietly, "Davis, I wish I did not love you so much."

Aunt Bell left a lasting memory as the lovingest, caringest, huggingest, most generous aunt ever. Would you believe that I was out of the country and missed her funeral? They said it was the biggest, saddest, happiest funeral in the county.

7

Tweenlight

On Gramby's front porch were two rocking chairs and a wide two-seater swing. I loved to sit on that swing and rock, kicking my feet out just enough to keep it moving. We often sat on the porch after dinner. Gramby brought out glasses of freshly made lemonade or sweet iced tea with mint picked from her mint patch by the back steps

Sometimes she ran a cord from the living room window so we could listen to the radio. Other times we might play a few hands of gin rummy. Most often we just talked and listened to the sounds in the garden at dusk and into the night.

Gramby said, "I love the tweenlight."

"What's tweenlight?"

"It's that time of day when the sun goes down but there's still light until it's fully dark."

"I thought that was called twilight."

"It is. That's what everyone else says, but my Mama called it tweenlight, and my grandma did too. I think she learned it from her grandma. So in *this* family that's what we say, Tweenlight. I think it fits. It's special to have a family word."

Tweenlight is the term I still use.

At tweenlight, a symphony was turned on in the garden. Crickets, toads, and frogs serenaded us. Wrens made their final calls before nesting for the night. Bees quieted down for the day, but you could still hear a buzz fading with the light. In the distance we heard the sweet song of a train whistle. An owl announced that it had taken its nightly position in a nearby tree. I heard that owl almost every night, but I was never able to catch so much as a glimpse of it the entire summer.

The lightning bugs began broadcasting their presence in Gramby's side garden at tweenlight. Lightning bugs are slow and even in the fading light were easy to catch. Gramby gave me a Mason jar to put my catches in after poking a few holes in the lid "so they can breathe." Most evenings I caught several dozen before I grew tired of the chase. I took that jar to bed with me and watched it glow on my bedside table. I let them go in the morning, but not many lived through the night.

We were sitting on the porch one evening and a light rain began to fall. I became aware of a pleasing sweet odor with the first rain.

"What is that smell?" I said. "Do you smell it?"

"Yes. I know that smell, and it comes when the rain starts. My grandma told me it was caused by the dust getting damp."

"It's a wonderful smell. Does it last long?"

"After a while in a longer rain it goes away, but I love that smell that hangs around after a short shower. Maybe someday you"ll learn about it when you take a science class."

"I don't think I'll ever forget it; it's nice."

"They say you never forget a smell like fresh rain on dust, or leaves decomposing in the woods, or freshly cut grass. Those smells will stay with you forever."

She was right. I still recognize that smell and remember the first time I was aware of it. I like the rain on dust explanation.

One tweenlight after a shower started, Gramby started singing *I Get the Blues when it Rains.*

"That's a sad song," I said. "But I like it; why don't you sing it again." And she did, many times over the summer.

"I first heard it back in the '20's when your Daddy was just a boy," she said. "Your grandfather and I used to sit on this porch and sing that song. He played a guitar and sang a great tenor harmony. I think of him when I'm on this porch, especially when it rains. It reminds me once again how much I miss him. It means a lot to have you here with me, Charles, and I'm glad you like that song."

That was the first of many musical evenings on the porch. "Rainy Blues" is what I called the song, and it was usually the first one I asked her to sing. It may have been the first song I ever learned, except for *Jesus Loves Me* and some other ones we sang at Sunday School. She started out and I would join in. She tried to teach me harmony, and it took a lot of trials and a lot of laughing before I finally grasped what harmony was about.

Gramby loved to sing, and she taught me many songs that continue to bring sweet memories: *Carolina Moon, Bye-bye Blackbird, Five Foot Two, You Must Have Been a Beautiful Baby, The Wabash Cannonball, Ain't She Sweet, Comin' Around the Mountain,* and *That Good Old Mountain Dew.* She knew all the verses to *The Wreck of the Old 97.*

We had fun making up verses to *Comin' Around the Mountain.* My best contribution, in my humble opinion, was *"She'll be bringing Gramby's biscuits when she comes."*

My children grew up making up verses to *Comin' Around the Mountain* and singing those songs...on trips in the car, at the beach, and around a campfire.

By the end of the summer I knew most of Gramby's songs by heart. It is rare to hear them anymore, but when I do, it takes me back to Gramby's front porch, back and forth in her swing, singing "Rainy Blues," catching lightning bugs, that owl, and rain on dust at tweenlight.

8

Judge Tacitus Law

Tacitus Law was a retired judge who lived in one of Aunt Bell's apartments. He had presided over the county court for over thirty years. Folks in Coldbrook considered him one of the truly upright citizens of the community.

Despite his fine reputation, Gramby said she thought Judge Law was a lonely man. He had no children to brighten his later years, and his wife's death left him alone. He sold his big, four-column brick house on North Main Street and moved into the Hotel Grover. He found respite from his loneliness by assuming a role as a member of Aunt Bell's family. He used her front lobby as his parlor. No matter who was there he sat down and joined the gathering. It became natural that he be involved, invited or not. In time he essentially adopted himself into our family and was included in family events.

Regardless of the time of day he always wore a high collar and bow tie. Aunt Bell told me he took great pride in his bow tie collection. She said he had a specific one for every day of the week plus special ones for weddings and funerals. "He never wears the same one two days in a row."

I saw Judge Law frequently at Aunt Bell's hotel. He seemed happy to chat with me, and I looked forward to those conversations. I asked him many questions about being a judge and how he made decisions. He said being a judge was dealing with the consequences of people's mistakes and crimes. He kept stressing the idea of consequences. He said most people who get into trouble with the law do so because they don't think through their actions and what can happen. "You eat too many ears of corn, you get sick."

He said it was the same in life. "Everything we do in life has consequences, some trivial, some good, some bad. It's the bad ones…the ones we don't think about…that get us in trouble…with a parent, a teacher, a team mate…or the law."

"Sometimes people made terrible mistakes and ended in front of me in court. I learned on the bench that I had to consider the consequences of *my* decisions." He gave one example.

"It was the first drunk driving case I heard, back about 1914 when driving an automobile was a relatively new experience for most folks. A local man got drunk and drove his car off the road and demolished a carriage and killed a horse. It would have been easy to just throw the man in jail, but I had to consider the consequences of my decision. If I put him in jail, would that help the owner get a new carriage and horse if the man couldn't work? Or what about his wife and children? Who would bring home money to pay for food and rent?"

"What did you do?"

"I gave him a suspended sentence, put him on probation for six months, and directed him to pay for a new carriage and horse. That way he could continue working and keep his family together."

"That seems fair."

"There were cases…robbery and such…when I had to sentence the guilty person to jail. The sad part in most of those cases was that it was the families of the criminals who had to bear the consequences as well. Too many times the mistakes we make cause problems for others."

"Because we don't think of the consequences."

"It looks like you understand what I've been trying to say. I hope you remember these stories when you grow older and take a job, and learn to drive, or have a family."

When he learned of my interest in baseball, we were rarely together that he didn't turn the conversation in that direction. He said he played baseball as a young man, second base, until he went to Law School. He didn't keep playing, he said, "because I couldn't hit a curve ball."

"I've been a baseball fan ever since I was a boy." He told me about how he became a Yankees fan in the 1920's when he went to New York on business and got tickets to a Yankees game. He caught a foul ball and got Babe Ruth and Lou Gehrig to sign it after the game. He said he thought that Yankee team was the best team ever. Being a Yankee fan in a small southern town wasn't popular; most of the locals seemed to root for the Cardinals.

"Now all I can do is just read about them, but I'm still a Yankee fan. I love Joe DiMaggio, but I must admit that I think Ted Williams is the best player now."

I didn't know he had a collection of autographed baseballs and was surprised when he offered to show them to me. Each one was in a small wooden box, and he wrapped them in tissue paper and then with a linen handkerchief. "I keep them wrapped this way so they won't fade." Besides Babe Ruth and Lou Gehrig, he showed me balls signed by Walter Johnson and Dizzy Dean. "I have a few more I'll show you later," he said.

During my second year in college I received a small box in the mail from Aunt Bell. She included a note that said Judge Law had died "and he asked me to send this to you. He said he knew you would appreciate and keep it safe."

Inside was a baseball, wrapped in tissue and a linen handkerchief.

It was autographed by Babe Ruth and Lou Gehrig.

9

Eloise Patterson

Miss Eloise Patterson was one of Gramby's oldest friends. "Miss Pat," as everyone in Coldbrook called her, was the town librarian. Gramby went regularly to the library and one day said in her accustomed style, "Why don't we go to the library today."

I was not sure what to expect, but as usual I went along. Gramby said, "You will like the librarian. We are dear friends; I have known her for a long time. We were in school together and came to Coldbrook at the same time. She is one of my bridge partners."

"What's bridge?"

"It's a card game I like to play, but I've given it up for the summer so I can be with you. You are certainly more important than a card game."

"You could go if you wanted to. It's all right with me. I'd be okay."

"No, I'm happy being with you. Maybe later I will teach you how to play gin rummy. It's a fun card game just the two of us could play. It was your grandfather's favorite."

"Sounds like a good idea. Let's do it."

The library was a small brick building on the grounds of the Coldbrook elementary school. When we arrived, Gramby introduced me to Miss Pat. The two of them shared stories while I looked around. There was a display of books with the title "New York Times Best Seller List Top Ten," and another with "New Books." It didn't look like there would be anything there for me.

Miss Pat said, "Are you interested in sports?"

"Sure, especially baseball. I can't believe you have books here about baseball."

"Come with me."

I followed her to an area of the library that had books for young people. She showed me a group of books, and said, "These are all about different sports, including baseball. I'll bet you can find one you like."

The title of the first book I picked up was *Cracker Stanton*, and it had a picture on the cover of a ball player swinging a bat. Little did I realize then that Cracker Stanton would become one of my heroes. I thumbed through it enough to see it was indeed a baseball story, so I took it to the desk and asked Miss Pat to check it out for me. Gramby said I could use her library card.

"Why don't we get a card for you. You can come back when you want if you decide you would like to get another book," she said.

Miss Pat said, "That's a good idea. I will have one for you when you finish the book and bring it back."

Cracker Stanton turned out to be a special young man. He was the best player on his Brentwood school team, was a great teammate, encouraged the other boys on the team, and always displayed top sportsmanship. At the end of the story his team was battling its arch rival Westerling for the championship. There were two outs in the bottom of the ninth. Brentwood trailed by two runs when Cracker Stanton came to bat with two men on. The count was three balls, two strikes. Cracker Stanton hit the next pitch to right field. The fielder went back, leaped, and watched the ball clear the fence just over his glove. That had to be a perfect ending to a great story. I had a new hero.

I finished that book in about a day. I couldn't put it down. Gramby had to call me several times to set the table for dinner, because I wanted to read just one more chapter, one more page, one more paragraph.

The next day I rode my bike to the library to return *Cracker Stanton*.

Miss Pat said, "You finished that book in a hurry. That must mean you liked it; would you like to try another one?"

"Sure."

"Well, I think you know where to look. Let me know if you can't find a book you like."

I went back to the area where I found *Cracker Stanton* and there were six more sports books by the same writer. They were about baseball, football, and basketball. Before the summer was over I read another baseball story, two about football, and one about basketball. I had never played football or basketball, so reading those books got me interested in those sports as well as baseball.

Miss Pat showed me more books by that same writer. They were about airplanes and the young heroes who flew them: Bill Bolton, Naval Aviator, and Great Ace Billy Smith. I read one book in each of those series and wrote down the titles of all of them so I could read them when I got home after the summer.

I became a frequent visitor to the library on my way uptown or to play baseball. On one of my trips I stopped by the library to drop off a Bill Bolton book, and Miss Pat said she thought she had found other books I might find interesting. "A lot of the boys in town like these, and I thought you would too."

She handed me a book entitled *The Royal Road to Romance*. I thumbed through it and saw interesting pictures of places around the world. Everything I saw was new to me.

The Royal Road to Romance was about the exploits of a young American named Richard Halliburton. In it he recounted his adventures flying around the world with an aviator friend in a biplane in Europe, Africa, and Asia. This became another book I couldn't put down. I soon followed it with four others I read in which Halliburton wrote about his exploits:

A Book of Marvels, The Glorious Adventure, New Worlds to Conquer, and *Seven League Boots.*

Richard Halliburton did incredible things. He recounted in his books his visits to Timbuktu, the French Foreign Legion in Algeria, Suez, Baghdad, Persia, the Taj Mahal, and the Mongolian desert. He swam the entire length of the Panama Canal. He flew across the Sahara Desert in Africa and other deserts in Asia. He walked on the Great Wall of China. He climbed to Machu Picchu in Peru. He met famous people in country after country. He flew around Mt. Everest in his biplane taking pictures. In his books there were hundreds of accounts of his travels, each one captivating. One of my favorites was about his being lifted in a basket up a sheer cliff to visit a monastery in Greece. It was the only access to that ancient place.

I found out later that Richard Halliburton had died. It was reported that he set out from Hong Kong in 1939 in a Chinese junk with the goal of reaching California and sailing, with appropriate fanfare, under the new Golden Gate bridge. The junk disappeared at sea without a trace, and Richard Halliburton was lost to the world...and me.

He lives on for me, however, in his books.

To say that the books of Richard Halliburton captured my imagination that summer would be an understatement. They painted a picture of a great world out there, a world with fascinating places to visit and wondrous things to see. Here was another hero for me. Could I make those kinds of journeys around the world? Could I meet those people? Could I visit exotic places and send back reports and photographs for others to see for the first time? I did dream about doing just that.

Is that why I joined the Navy?

Reading Richard Halliburton's books gave me a lifelong interest in world geography and travel to foreign lands. Many years later I was in Japan and saw the Great Buddha of Kamakura. I couldn't help but think about Richard Halliburton. Was I standing in the same spot he did when

BACON GREASE & BASEBALL

he visited here? Did I report the same impressions? the same excitement? Did I take the same photographs?

I thought about Miss Pat and how grateful I am to her for introducing me to books that gave me such inspiring heroes--Cracker Stanton and Richard Halliburton. One made his mark following the rules; the other seemed to pride himself in breaking them.

I'm also grateful to Miss Pat for giving me my first library card. I have never been without one.

10

Mayor Wallace

Frank "Buddy" Wallace was the Mayor of Coldbrook. He was an important lawyer in town and the father of my baseball friend Matt. Gramby said Mayor Wallace had his nose in almost everyone's business in Coldbrook. That's probably why he kept getting elected.

What I liked about Mayor Wallace was his Model A Ford. He was usually seen around town in that beautiful automobile. Most Model A's then were black, but Mayor Wallace had his painted a deep maroon with yellow spoked wheels. It had a tan canvas top, polished chrome fittings, and, best of all, a rumble seat.

He loved to drive with the top down, and he let Matt bring a bunch of his baseball buddies for rides. Mayor Wallace was known to take a few extra turns around town when the boys were in the car.

The prime spot in the Model A was the rumble seat; that's where everyone wanted to sit. I thought I was pretty lucky those times when it was my turn to ride in the rumble seat. The most fun was to drive through the country with friends piled in a rumble seat and the wind blowing in our faces.

I decided a Ford Model A was definitely the automobile I had to have when I got old enough to drive, a Model A just like Mayor Wallace's. That hasn't worked out for me, but I still want one.

Gramby once said, "Buddy Wallace is a good Mayor; he gets them to pick up the trash every week."

11

Saturday at the Movies

Thad and Stubby came by early Saturday morning the first weekend I was in Coldbrook. Thad said, "Come on, Charlie. You've got to go with us to the movies; it's Western day. They show Westerns all day long and everybody goes."

Gramby had apparently been warned by Mrs. Haymore about Saturday at the movies. I was surprised when she had no questions, needed no explanation, and was ready to give me the money for the ticket and extra for popcorn and a drink. "Come right home after the movie," she said. "Enjoy."

I don't think she realized how long that was going to be. That first day I didn't either. In the following weeks she usually sent me off to the movies on Saturday with a bag lunch. "We have to hurry and get there early," Thad said. "We don't want to let someone else get our seats." We hopped on our bikes and headed uptown.

The movie theater in Gramby's town was small with just one center aisle. It may have been the only one in America to have a special lineup each Saturday that included *three* full length Westerns. Between each feature was a newsreel or Pete Smith Specialties, a cartoon, and an action serial. That amounted to more than six hours of entertainment, and, for twenty-five cents (including popcorn), it was a deal calculated to make a boy happy each week...and to fill up the theater.

Boys made up most of the audience, some of whom I had met on the ball field that week. Shorty and Lance arrived at the ticket booth the same time we did and joined us. Lance still had on the same grungy shirt he wore on the ball field the day I met him; Stubby brought that to everyone's attention when he shouted, "Nice shirt, Lancelot." It was, of course, followed by a number of other comments, better left unreported. Thad led us down front to seats in the fourth row. "This is where we always sit," he said. "They are the best seats in the house." I don't know if there were better seats in the theater because Row Four Right is where we sat the rest of the summer. Even now, I gravitate to that part of a theater when I go to the movies.

A few girls also showed up. Jimbo's sister Sarah was one of the regulars. She and Nancy Shorter and Chickie Frye tried to sit in the row behind us each week. Did they like westerns, or did they enjoy pestering us? Thad tried to get other boys to take those seats before the girls could get there, but the girls usually won that ongoing Saturday battle. They spent the entire summer annoying us. I asked Thad why we didn't just find other seats, but he said "You can't let those stupid girls run us out these seats. These are the best. And besides they'd just follow us."

The movies featured the great Western stars of the day: Roy Rogers and Dale Evans, Gene Autry, Wild Bill Hickock, the Cisco Kid, the Lone Ranger, and more. Most of the stars had a "sidekick" who appeared with them in their movies, and I grew to love Gabby Hayes, Smiley Burnett, Pancho, Slim Pickens, and Tonto. Their voices are deeply implanted in my memory. I close my eyes and can still hear Gabby's drawling "Roy," and Smiley's whining "Aw, Gene."

I loved the serials. Each one had from ten to twelve episodes of about 15 minutes each and was designed to keep the customers coming back. At the end of each episode the hero or his sidekick or his lady friend was apparently killed or captured or shot in that chapter's last scene. "Come next week to see the next thrilling chapter of ...." The next episode opened with that same scene, but this time it had been re-photographed, and our hero made it out of the death-defying predicament to fight for another fifteen minutes.

I saw only one serial from beginning to end. Hopalong Cassidy eventually shot up the gang trying to take over the Carver ranch, saved the beautiful young Carver daughter Angelina, and rode off into the sunset with his partner Andy Clyde. I was only able to see half of the episodes of the other serials playing that summer. I saw either the beginning or ending episodes of Wild Bill Hickock, The Royal Mounted Police, Red Ryder, Golden Arrow, and Zorro. Those serials had started before I began going to the movies with the boys on Saturday or ended after I left Coldbrook at the end of the summer.

One of the problems with six hours of uninterrupted entertainment is that young boys have to go to the bathroom. Imagine coming back to find that you missed the *Tom and Jerry* cartoon because of the long line at the bathroom. They said it was the best one ever, so the temptation was intense to see the whole cycle over to catch that cartoon. Many a Saturday ended for a young boy with an irate mother walking up and down the aisle calling for her son to come home to dinner. Gramby made a point of telling me, "You come home on time; I don't want to have to go uptown and drag you out of that theater." She never had to.

A summer of Saturdays at the movies with a triple feature and my baseball buddies made me a Western movie fan for life.

I never did find out how Little Beaver got Red Ryder out of that abandoned silver mine before it blew up, but I am sure that he did.

12

Buttermilk Biscuits

It didn't take me long to fall in love with Gramby's buttermilk biscuits. She served them almost every dinner, and I could never get enough of them. On the rare occasion that there were a few left over, I made sure to finish them off the next day.

I wanted to see how she made them and during my first week with her I asked, "Why don't we make more of those good biscuits?"

"I was getting ready to do that anyway, so you will have to watch carefully. I'll let you help."

She put flour in a bowl with other dry ingredients, took butter out of the refrigerator and cut it into small pieces, put that into the flour with a dollop of bacon grease, and then poured in the buttermilk.

"We have to mix this together softly; the less we handle it the fluffier the biscuit."

She sprinkled flour on the counter and with her hands spread the dough out until it was just under a half inch thick. I leaned up against the counter, watching closely and getting flour on my shirt.

"Why don't you use a rolling pin?"

"Using a rolling pin just makes the biscuits tougher. My grandma taught me how to make them, and she said you have to treat them gently, like a little baby. I try to handle the dough as little as I can, just press it out with my fingers enough to get it to the right thickness."

She took a biscuit cutter and showed me how to dip it in flour, press firmly, shake it to loosen a biscuit from the rest of the dough, and then place it on a baking sheet. She let me do the rest of them. When we had cut them out, she pulled the scraps back together, pressed it out again, and we were able to get another three or four biscuits. She brushed the tops of each one with melted butter and said, "Why don't we let them rest while the oven heats."

With the biscuits in the oven, a wonderful aroma filled the kitchen. After a few minutes she opened the oven and out came beautiful, puffy biscuits. She let them cool for a few more minutes and then said, "Why don't we try one right now while they are still warm. Put on a pat of butter and some honey...or maybe grape jam."

I became an instant fan of Gramby's buttermilk biscuits, and I spent the summer dreaming up new ways to eat those biscuits. I decided that anything that is good in a sandwich would taste much better in one of her biscuits. Over the summer I "invented:"

-peanut butter and jelly in a buttermilk biscuit

-bacon in a buttermilk biscuit

-peanut butter and slices of banana in a buttermilk biscuit

-ham in a buttermilk biscuit

-ham and cheese in a buttermilk biscuit

-sausage in a buttermilk biscuit

-ham and cheese and bacon in a buttermilk biscuit

I decided I needed bigger biscuits for my inventions and asked Gramby, "Can we use a larger biscuit cutter?" She found one, and my creative efforts expanded.

-sliced chicken, white or dark, in a buttermilk biscuit

-sliced tomato and bacon in a buttermilk biscuit

-bacon, lettuce and tomato in a buttermilk biscuit

-scrambled egg and bacon or sausage in a buttermilk biscuit

-cucumber pickles in a buttermilk biscuit

-chicken salad in a buttermilk biscuit

-fried egg in a buttermilk biscuit

I first used mayonnaise on a lot of my biscuits, but Gramby suggested, "Why don't we try a bit of mustard as well." That added a whole new flavor to my creations. I learned that some biscuits tasted better with mayo, some with mustard, and some with both. I could add bacon to almost anything.

-thick slice of tomato and a thick slice of onion in a buttermilk biscuit

-pimento cheese in a buttermilk biscuit

-sliced apple and peanut butter in a buttermilk biscuit

-thin slices of raw zucchini in a buttermilk biscuit

-sliced cucumbers in a buttermilk biscuit

-sliced strawberries in a buttermilk biscuit

-corned beef in a buttermilk biscuit

-sliced strawberries and honey in a buttermilk biscuit

A whole new creative potential was born. I kept getting new ideas and Gramby kept me supplied with buttermilk biscuits.

-roast beef in a buttermilk biscuit

-tuna salad in a buttermilk biscuit

-Vienna sausage in a buttermilk biscuit

-slices of steak or pork in a buttermilk biscuit

-chipped beef in a buttermilk biscuit

-mushrooms and onions, fried in bacon grease, in a buttermilk biscuit

-spam in a buttermilk biscuit

I shared my biscuit creations with Thad and Stubby, and they began to ask me to bring them along to our ball games. Stubby said, "You could sell these and make a million. Everybody would buy them."

"I can't imagine that anyone would buy biscuits like these," I said. "There are too many restaurants selling *good* food. And besides, I would rather be playing baseball than working in a kitchen all day."

Selling biscuits for a living? An idea whose time had not yet come. I left my millions for somebody else to make.

I could never think of a way to use black-eyed peas.

13

Sadie and Ella Whiteside

Miss Sadie and Miss Ella Whiteside lived a few doors toward town from Gramby's house. She always spoke of them as "those sweet Whiteside sisters." We often visited at their home over the summer, and I came to enjoy those times with the ladies. They engaged me in conversation and treated me like a friend, not just a tag-along grandson.

Miss Sadie was Principal of Coldbrook Elementary School, had been for over thirty years. She may have been the best known and most revered person in town as almost everyone in Coldbrook under thirty-five or forty had been to her school. She knew most of their parents. Gramby enjoyed getting together with her and talking...talk about old times, and how things had changed, and how it was so much better when they were young. They also reviewed the latest happenings on the radio soap operas they liked. Miss Sadie loved to talk. I looked forward to those visits because I always learned something interesting, something I didn't know about the "good old days."

Miss Sadie was a reliable source for what was going on in town. She was also a source for fresh vegetables and eggs which she liked to share with her neighbors and friends. The "sweet Whiteside sisters" raised chickens and vegetables, growing things like corn, tomatoes, beans, peas, squash, cucumbers...and *watermelon!* She regularly sent vegetables to us as her things ripened. Miss Sadie told me she saved seeds each summer to start her plants the following year. She said the seeds were passed down for several generations in her family. Her grandmother had started the garden when she was a new bride. Eating Miss Sadie's tomatoes made me a home-grown tomato lover forever and gave me an appreciation for what we now call heirloom tomatoes. Now I look for old timey tomatoes at the Farmers' Market when I go.

Miss Ella was a different person. She was the primary housekeeper and caretaker for their aging mother. When I first saw Mother Whiteside, I thought she must be the oldest person in the world. When we visited, she just sat there in her chair with a blank look, pale, drawn and fragile, warmed by a blanket even in August. She neither smiled nor frowned nor spoke. The first time I went to the Whiteside house with Gramby, trying to be polite, I spoke to her. I was put off when she ignored me. When I later asked Gramby about it, she said not to mind Mother Whiteside, just say something nice and forget about it. "It will make Miss Sadie happy."

I didn't understand why Miss Ella said nothing either. Then I learned that she was deaf. Gramby told me later that she had been born that way and had gone to a special school for the deaf as a girl.

Miss Ella used her hands to make the letters of the alphabet to "talk." Over the summer she taught me how to "talk on my hands." Gradually I learned each letter, and soon I was talking with Miss Ella. She seemed especially pleased whenever I came around and began testing me. I could never seem to remember how to sign the letter "P." Why "P" of all the letters in the alphabet? Why not "X," which was not used very much in English? The sign for "X" was easy to remember.

I was pleased to go back to school with a new skill that no one else in my class would have. It certainly helped me become a better speller.

One afternoon Miss Sadie called to ask me to come over and pick up a "mess of black-eyed peas" for Gramby. When I arrived, she was sitting at her kitchen table cleaning a hen. She had already pulled the feathers and was working on the internals, what Gramby called "the giblets." Miss Sadie showed me the heart, the liver, and the gizzard, all of which she explained would be cooked or used to make "giblet gravy." In time I surprised myself by learning to like those giblets, particularly chicken livers.

It fascinated me when she removed a long tube from the interior of the hen. Visible throughout the length of the tube were egg yolks, some two dozen of them. At one end a yolk was tiny, no larger than the head of a pin, but clearly recognizable as a miniature yolk. As my eyes followed along the tube, I could see that the yolks became progressively larger until, at the end of the tube, the yolk was full size. Miss Sadie explained the yolk was then ready for the shell to be secreted and an egg laid. She said the yolks were all edible; she planned to have some for breakfast...sunny side up...and use them for puddings and cakes.

All this...the giblets, the yolks in the long tube...was a revelation. It was my first lesson in anatomy.

Early in the summer Miss Ella stopped me when I was riding my bike home from baseball. I saw her standing in her front yard from a distance, and she appeared to be looking for something or someone. That turned out to be me.

"C-A-N Y-O-U H-E-L-P M-E," she asked, signing. "Y-E-S," I responded as I jumped off the bike.

"F-O-L-L-O-W," she signed and started immediately around the side of her house.

"B-E-E-S S-W-A-R-M E-V-E-R-Y Y-E-A-R."

I wasn't excited about getting involved with bees. I had not yet learned that bees were harmless to humans in almost all circumstances. Gramby had told me to "just leave them alone and they will do the same," but that "almost" kept me moving around the side of the house with caution.

Miss Ella led me to a tall evergreen cedar tree on one side of the vegetable garden and pointed to a football sized dark blob on the tree. Countless bees were buzzing about the blob; I stood my distance.

"S-W-A-R-M-I-N-G," she signed. "L-O-O-K-I-N-G F-O-R A P-L-A-C-E T-O S-E-T-T-L-E."

"W-H-A-T C-A-N I D-O?"

"F-O-L-L-O-W M-E."

She led me to her garage and pointed out a white wooden box and motioned for me to pick it up. "H-I-V-E," she signed. She picked up a folding table and we returned to the swarming bees on the cedar tree. She put on a hat with a net over it that covered her face. I was nervous about what was about to take place, but she put a hat with a net on my head and smiled. It made me feel only a bit better.

Back in the garden Miss Ella unfolded the table and placed it next to the cedar tree and motioned for me to put the hive on the table. She handed me a thick stick. "U-S-E I-T W-H-E-N I T-E-L-L Y-O-U." She reached up with a hoe to catch the branch with the swarm and pulled it down until the swarm was over the table. She pointed to a spot on the branch and signed, "H-I-T I-T."

I gave it my homerun swing, hit the branch as hard as I could, and jumped back ready to run when the bees attacked.

The swarm fell to the table, a mass of bees, struggling, moving, climbing over each other.

"O K."

After a few minutes she began tapping rhythmically on the back of the hive, and, what was amazing, the bees began marching into the hive through an opening in the front. It was as if they were marching in cadence. "F-O-L-L-O-W-I-N-G T-H-E Q-U-E-E-N," she explained. When most of the bees had entered, a few remained flying about the area over the table. A deep buzzing sound came from within the hive. I still kept my distance.

Miss Ella stood back, smiled at me, and signed, "T-H-A-N-K-S. W-I-L-L Y-O-U C-O-M-E B-A-C-K T-H-I-S E-V-E. H-E-L-P M-O-V-E T-H-E H-I-V-E."

"Y-E-S. W-H-A-T T-I-M-E."

"S-E-V-E-N. B-E-E-S W-I-L-L B-E C-A-L-M T-H-E-N."

When I got home I described the adventure with the bees to Gramby and said I had to eat early enough to help Miss Ella at seven. She told me the Whiteside sisters often kept bees. She said with all the clover and honey suckle in the neighborhood, they usually make some delicious honey. "And I'm sure Miss Ella will give you some."

When Miss Ella and I returned to the hive, it was quiet, although I could still hear buzzing, audible but quieter. There were no scouts flying about, which made me feel safer. She thanked me for coming and motioned for me to carry the hive to the far edge of the vegetable garden where there was a stand for it. I had to put on my bravery face, as I was nervous thinking about all those bees right next to my body.

The bees were indeed calm. Miss Ella knew what she was doing. I placed the hive on the stand, stood back, and felt very proud of myself.

Again she thanked me and signed, "V-E-R-Y B-R-A-V-E." I was relieved...and happy.

She went in the house and came out with a jar she gave me.

"F-R-O-M L-A-S-T Y-E-A-R." She smiled, gave me a hug, and thanked me again.

The next morning, I enjoyed "sweet" Miss Ella Whiteside's clover honey on three of Gramby's buttermilk biscuits.

Now whenever I can "talk on my hands," I try to avoid words that have "P" in them. I realize that I will always have to sign "P-L-E-A-S-E." I do remember the letters for "H-O-N-E-Y."

Knowing how to talk on my hands was not all biscuits and honey. Miss Ella had also taught Gramby how to do it. If we were somewhere and I started to talk about something I shouldn't, I noticed that Gramby, without drawing attention

- closed her hand into a fist and put her thumb over her middle two fingers: S

- moved her thumb between her first and second finger: T

- opened her fist slightly and put her thumb on her first finger: O

She didn't need to get to P.

14

Harley Wimbush

Of all the boys who played baseball with me in Coldbrook, Harley Wimbush was the hardest to like. He always seemed to be in a bad mood. He argued balls and strikes. He insisted he was safe even when he was out by a mile. Foul balls always fell to his advantage. He yelled and cussed at anyone, on any occasion. The boys put up with him because they always needed players, but the way he acted put him right on the verge of being outright disliked.

Harley was usually one of the last chosen when we divided up. He wasn't a good ball player, but he almost always showed up at Coldbrook Field when we played.

I came close to getting into a fight with Harley.

We rarely had enough boys to fill two teams, so we had to improvise to have an umpire behind the plate to call balls and strikes and on the field to call the bases. And, of course, there were not enough to have coaches at first and third.

In years of playing at Coldbrook Field boys had come up with a workable solution, passed from generation to generation of young ball players. The team at bat would provide one of its players to ump behind the plate and two at first and third to both coach and umpire. As it became their time to bat, another player would slide into the role. Because everyone at one time was both player and umpire, honesty prevailed. No one cheated because no one wanted to be cheated.

My dustup with Harley happened when I called him out on an easy play at third base. He jumped up and screamed at me that he was safe. He yelled and said I was blind and that I was a cheat and that I didn't belong in Coldbrook and should go back to the city where I belonged.

I said, "Harley, you were out."

He lunged at me with his arm cocked. He would probably have hit me if Jimbo hadn't grabbed him.

By then other boys gathered around. Matt and Tommy moved to stand between us, and Matt said, "OK, Harley, settle down."

The other boys told Harley to knock it off. "Let's play ball."

Harley was still seething when I came back to bat but said nothing more. I noticed that Thad and Shorty made a point of standing near me the rest of the afternoon. They were keeping an eye on Harley.

After the game, Harley looked at me with hate in his eyes but left without saying a word.

I didn't know what to expect. Would Harley try to fight me the next time we played? Thad told me not to worry. "It's just Harley. He's always mad at something or somebody. He does nothing about it."

When I got home, I found Gramby in the kitchen shelling lima beans Miss Sadie had brought over. I ate a black strap cookie and helped her with the beans.

After a while, Gramby said, "You're awfully quiet. Is everything all right?"

I told her about Harley and what he said and how upset I was about it.

"I thought he would punch me, but some of the other boys stepped in and stopped him. He was stupid to get that worked up about being called out. He *was* out, but Harley's always arguing calls that go against him. I think none of the other boys like to play with him because of it. I don't know what's wrong with Harley. He's a mess."

69

"I think Harley has a very hard time at home. That's probably why Harley...and Hector for that matter...are like they are."

"What's wrong at their home?"

"Their father, Homer Wimbush, is a bitter man. He works as a mechanic at the Esso station. He has a reputation as a good mechanic but someone who is very difficult to get along with. He always seems to be angry at something, anything, anybody. I don't think I've ever seen him smile. It must impact his boys."

"Why is he like that?"

"When Homer Wimbush came home from the war, he came home with a steel plate in his head where part of his skull should be. He lost an ear and an eye. He was badly wounded and, given his head wounds, is lucky to be alive. He's never seemed to be able to make peace with his condition and move on with his life. When he got home he found out his wife had run off and left him to raise those two boys. It can't be easy for him. He's so bitter."

"I can see what that may have done for Harley and Hector, but I don't know what to do about Harley the next time I see him."

"You have two choices. You can yell at each other for the rest of the summer and maybe come to blows or you can decide to forgive him and treat him nicely. I always say, 'Kill 'em with kindness.' You just might gain a friend. It sounds like Harley could use a good friend. How would you like to be treated?"

I went to bed that night thinking about Harley and Hector and their Dad in the war. I wondered what I would feel like if it were me. If Daddy had been wounded like that? What would I do? What should I do?

The next day I rode my bike with Thad and Stubby to Coldbrook Field, worried about a confrontation with Harley.

When we got there, they told us it was my turn to be one of the team captains that day and choose up sides. Harley hung about on the edge of the crowd, looking angry. Thad and I did fist over fist on a bat to see who would pick first. I had the last solid grip, and then Thad tried to kick the bat out of my hand. I held on and had first choice.

"I choose Harley." Thad looked at me like I was crazy. I repeated, "I choose Harley."

Years later, at Gramby's funeral, a man came up to me with a big smile on his face. He put his hand on my shoulder, shook my hand warmly, and said, "I'm Harley. I was hoping I would get a chance to talk to you."

"Thanks, Harley. What are you doing now? Do you still live in Coldbrook?"

"Yeah. Still in Coldbrook. My Daddy taught me how to fix cars. Since I finished high school I've been doing auto work."

We traded information about our families and I said, "Is Hector still here?"

"No, he drives a bus for Greyhound and lives over in Bedford."

Harley said, "I sure am sorry about your grandma. She was a fine lady. I saw her a lot around town, and she was always so nice to me. She knew we were good friends so she kept me up to date on what you were doing. I know you will miss her."

"I will."

"That summer you were here, that was a lot of fun, playing baseball and all."

"Yes it was, Harley. It sure was."

15

Radio

Gramby had four radios, and at least one of them was going all the time. She loved the soaps, and I soon became familiar with many of her daily listening choices of *Lorenzo Jones, Ma Perkins, Pepper Young's Family, Mary Noble Backstage Wife*, and what was her favorite, *Stella Dallas*. I often asked her at dinner what was the latest crisis on her soaps, and she responded with great detail. They packed a lot of drama in those fifteen-minute programs (and sold a lot of soap) and left you on edge so you won't miss the next episode.

I had a radio in my room and developed my own group of favorites, broadcast I am sure for boys. The four o'clock hour began the best time of day. There was a series of exciting programs I tried not to miss. It started with the adventures of *Jack Armstrong, the All-American Boy*, who was followed by *Don Winslow of the Navy, Captain Midnight*, and *Red Ryder*. I thought of those radio people as old friends.

The next hour began with my absolute favorite, *The Lone Ranger*, who rid the west of bad men, accompanied by his faithful Indian companion, Tonto. At the end of each episode, The Lone Ranger left a silver bullet and could be heard as he rode off with a hearty, "Hi-ho, Silver, away." Tonto rode with him with "Get-'em up, Scout," And then there was always a crowd left behind in which someone asked, "Who was that masked man?"

I didn't realize I was gaining an appreciation for classical music by listening to the theme songs of those programs. Many years later when

I heard Tchaikovsky, Rachmaninoff, Rossini, or Chopin, I thought, "*Oh, yeah, I recognize that from The Lone Ranger, or that one was from Road of Life.*"

Gramby knew how much that afternoon radio time meant to me and rarely called me away for some chore during that time. She did call me when a guest came by. She wanted me to be present to greet guests and join in the conversation. She spent most of her Saturday afternoons listening to the Metropolitan Opera in live broadcasts from New York. I didn't want to give up Saturday at the movies to listen, and I never became an opera fan.

We spent many evenings together listening to programs we both liked. We looked forward each week to *Your Hit Parade*. We shared opinions about which songs would be featured and were happy or sad when our favorite was or was not in the first place we thought it should be. We also shared a love for the radio comedies--Fred Allen, Jack Benny, Milton Berle, and others. Radio comedies had regular characters who came on each week for a short bit. The writers gave those characters special lines that became their unique trademarks and were repeated in each episode. We waited each week with anticipation to see how that special line would be included. One of my favorite characters was Digger O'Dell, "your friendly undertaker" on *Life of Riley*. His departing line was always, "I guess I'll be... shoveling off." I still think it's funny.

I usually finished my day in my room listening to the radio. The mystery stories grabbed my attention, most of which were designed to scare and frighten. They succeeded, but I listened to them anyway, *The Shadow*, *Lights Out*, *The Whistler*, and *Suspense*. The scariest was *Inner Sanctum*. It opened with the sound of a creaking door, and a story followed that made me pull the covers up and make sure the light was still burning. The announcer closed the show with a deep "Pleasant dreeeeeams," followed by the creaking door again. It did not make going to sleep easier. I still get a chill when I hear a creaking door.

The other thing I did in my room was wander throughout the radio world. I didn't understand the science that enabled me to listen to far away stations at night. I later learned that, based on geographic distance, the unique character of the upper atmosphere at night, and the power of a station's transmitter, you could pick up wonderful stations from all over the country if the AM signal "bounce" were right. I listened to stations in Chicago, St. Louis, Minneapolis, and Boston. I could occasionally catch a station in Cincinnati and listen to the Reds play a night game at Crosley Field. The Reds weren't very good that summer, but I learned a good bit about baseball strategy from the commentary.

I didn't care much for country music, but I enjoyed WCKY, a station in Cincinnati. It was the kind of station that played one song maybe every 15 or 20 minutes and spent the rest of the time trying to sell something. I didn't listen for the music (although sometimes they played an Eddie Arnold song I liked), but I found the ads amusing. They were directed toward farm listeners. I can hear that announcer now: "Yes, send $2.98... that's two dollars and ninety-eight cents...two nine eight...by money order with your name and address to Baby Chicks, that B-A-B-Y-C-H-I-C-K-S, care of WCKY, Cincinnati, Ohio, and get your dozen baby chicks by return mail."

On Sunday nights, if the bounce were right, I listened to WLW in New Orleans and discovered Dixieland jazz, beginning a lifelong love for that style of music. There was WTOP in Washington that played the top hits of the day from nine to midnight. I had to be careful to keep it quiet that late at night to keep Gramby from coming upstairs and shutting me down.

I came home from baseball one afternoon and went to the cookie tin and found Gramby ironing. She was listening to one of her soaps. She said, "It's nice to listen to the radio while I'm ironing. It's one of the best things about radio; I can iron, or sew, or wash dishes, or whatever and still keep up with the story. It doesn't interfere; I don't have to take my eyes off of what I'm doing; just listen."

"Why do you have to iron so much? You must to do it almost every day."

"Everything we wash comes out wrinkled. I want things to look right, and there is much to keep clean: clothes, bed linens, these napkins. I wouldn't want a nice young man like you going around wearing a wrinkled shirt and pants. What would your friends think?"

I thought about Lance.

I watched her ironing for a while, listening to the radio in the kitchen, and eating my second blackstrap cookie. "That looks like fun," I said.

"I'm not sure I would call it fun, but it's not hard and I find it relaxing. Why don't we teach you to iron," she said. "Let me show you how."

"First," she said, "you have to be careful. This iron is hot and it will burn you. If you put it down on the ironing board or on what you are ironing, you will scorch the ironing board cover too and ruin it. So let's try something easy. Why don't you hand me one of those napkins, and watch how I iron it."

She stretched a napkin on the ironing board, dipped her fingers in a bowl of water, sprinkled it over the napkin, and carefully went over it, pulling it out carefully so she didn't iron a crease into it.

"What is the water for?"

"Having a small amount of water on the cloth is like steaming it when the hot iron touches it."

This was years before she had a steam iron.

I thought it looked easy. "Can I try one?"

She smiled and handed me another napkin. I stretched it, sprinkled it, and gingerly applied the iron in what I thought were smooth strokes.

"Keep the iron moving. Never stop or you'll burn it."

I finished the napkin, put the iron on the holder, looked at the napkin, and felt good about myself. *"That wasn't too hard,"* I thought to myself. I didn't say that to Gramby.

"You did a nice job for your first try. We'll let you try a few more napkins so you can get confident in using the iron before we move on to other things."

Before long I graduated from napkins to handkerchiefs to dish towels to pillow cases. Then came the hard ones...shirts and pants. To get me ready to iron a shirt, she had me practice on pajamas. I took several weeks of trying before I could iron a shirt that met with Gramby's approval. I surprised myself by finding out that ironing gave me a feeling of having accomplished something when I hung up a nicely pressed shirt or pair of pants. It was okay on a rainy day, but not when it was nice and there was a game at Coldbrook field.

I had an idea I wanted to try. I took the top of a Mason jar and, with a nail, hammered a bunch of holes in the top. I filled the jar with water, screwed on the top, and gave it to Gramby. "Try this," I said. She used it to sprinkle the water on her ironing, and it worked. I didn't realize that I just had my first success at re-purposing. Of course, that word hadn't been invented yet. Gramby used my Mason jar sprinkler for her ironing for years until they came out with the steam iron. She told me even with her new steam iron, she always kept my sprinkler jar handy..."just in case."

This was a time before they developed wrinkle free materials, so there was a good deal of ironing to do. I think I helped Gramby a lot over the summer, and she always stayed around when I was ironing...in case I ran into a problem. We listened to a lot of soaps together. She even let me listen to *The Lone Ranger* while I was helping instead of *Stella Dallas*.

Knowing how to iron became a most valuable skill when I got married. I had to teach my new wife how to iron shirts and pants. I know how pleased she was when they came out with no-iron clothes and linens.

16

Virgil Mayfield

Officer Virgil Mayfield was a member of the small Coldbrook Police Department. There was not a lot of crime in town, so Officer Mayfield spent most of his time riding around in a squad car looking for trouble. His uncle had been on the force for many years, and Gramby said she thought that might have been the only reason they hired young Virgil Mayfield. She told me most of the Coldbrook policemen were well respected members of the community, but Officer Mayfield wasn't one. "He doesn't bring a lot of smarts to the table."

Officer Mayfield had a weight problem; his stomach hung over his belt. If one of his buttons popped, it looked like he might explode out of his uniform. Heat and stress made him perspire profusely; his uniform always showed stains. The younger town folks took great pleasure in making fun of him and gave him several nicknames over the years. My baseball buddies usually referred to him as Officer Sweatbox.

Gramby told me they almost fired Officer Mayfield his first week on the job. His first act as a new policeman was to give a ticket to a Trailways Bus driver for blocking traffic. The bus stopped next to the Courthouse, taking on or letting off passengers, the same spot Trailways used several times a day for decades.

Mr. Waterson told Gramby the regional manager for Trailways called Mayor Wallace and threatened to remove Coldbrook from all Trailways routes. Trailways buses were deeply woven into the fabric of Coldbrook life. The train provided long-distance travel north and south, but Trailways buses connected Coldbrook folks to surrounding towns and their rural families and friends. Loss of Trailways would have been devastating for the town. Mr. Waterson said Mayor Wallace apologized, assured Trailways it would never happen again, and said he would take care of the ticket. He also said Mayor Wallace had a heated conversation with the Sheriff about Officer Mayfield. The Sheriff was desperate for officers. It was during the war and few men were available for homeland duty. Virgil Mayfield could stay. The story raced around Coldbrook, and Officer Mayfield's reputation was low. It hadn't improved.

Gramby said, "Like him or not, he is a police officer and we should treat him with respect. It's best to stay out of his way."

A busy, important north-south highway ran right through the middle of town. Officer Mayfield was especially on the alert to protect the good citizens of Coldbrook from a speeding out-of-state automobile. Out-of-state drivers were his prey. His idea of speeding began at *one* mile per hour over the posted limit. Officer Mayfield also made sure to protect the citizens of Coldbrook from out-of-state drivers who did not make an absolutely complete halt at a stop sign. Three stop signs stood on the main road through town. When not otherwise involved in a police action, he staked out a position near one of those signs just out of view and waited for an out-of-state automobile or truck. This was a time before radar and speed guns, so Officer Mayfield's word ruled. A ticket would be written, a fine would be paid, and the luckless driver could then be on his way.

His favorite job involved leading a funeral procession from the church to the Coldbrook Memorial Cemetery, lights flashing and siren sounding at every intersection.

Officer Mayfield seemed to take great joy in harassing the boys in town. The adults wouldn't put up with him. If he came upon a group of us during his trips around town, he went through his routine. He sped up next to us, slammed on the brakes, made a big show of preparing to get out of the squad car, and then emerged with his hand on his holster and night stick in the other. Tapping the night stick menacingly in the palm of his hand, he said, "What are you boys up to?"

We answered in what became a timeless chorus in unison: "Nothing, Officer Mayfield, sir." With a big emphasis on the "sir." Shorty liked to lead the chorus, serving as our choir director.

"I can tell you are up to no good. Don't let me catch you doing stuff."

"Yes, Officer Mayfield, sir."

Officer Mayfield would once again go to each one in the group, shake his night stick in our faces, and say, "You'd better be glad I don't tell your father."

"Thank you, Officer Mayfield, sir."

Nobody's father ever heard from him about the awful things he caught us doing. Coldbrook was safer, but I wondered why Officer Sweatbox wasn't out there looking for all those men on the WANTED posters at the Post Office instead of waving his night stick in the faces of innocent boys.

17

Simon Parker's Horse Show

Simon Parker was a neighbor of Gramby's. He, his wife Evalina, and Simon, Jr. lived a few houses toward town on the other side of our street. Everyone called the son "Junior;" he was one of the kids who played baseball with us in Thad's cow pasture and Coldbrook Field.

Simon Parker was one of the fattest men I ever saw. He wasn't tall, but he was big, particularly around the middle. I wondered where he found pants that big and a belt that long. I understood why he always wore suspenders. I saw him frequently in his front yard or uptown at the New Food Emporium or the Post Office. On several occasions I saw him buy a six-bottle carton of Graveley's Tonic. When he walked, he looked like he was struggling to move, and, that once he got moving, he would be hard to stop. Gramby once said, "He's a man who knows how to have his cake and eat it too."

To look at his home from the street you wouldn't know he had a large complex behind the house with barns, support buildings, and grazing pastures filled with horses and cows. He also had a large riding ring with bleachers. Each summer Simon Parker hosted a regional horse show. Gramby said it was a big event in Coldbrook. Horse owners from long distances filled the town and surrounding area during the three days show to parade their finest. "It's good for local business."

Simon Parker made buildings available to groups interested in selling various horse show related items. Thad, Stubby and I had great fun roaming around the grounds, spending time with the stall people, learning where they were from, and listening to their pitches to customers. Hearing horse people talk introduced me to a whole new vocabulary, one I still can hardly understand. Every item had a special name. Most were new to me. The array of things for sale was amazing. I had no idea there was so much "horse stuff."

Vendors arrived in trailers loaded with saddles, bridles, stirrups, bits, harness, leather and woven straps of all shapes and sizes, whips and crops. There was a boot stall that featured Western and English riding boots and dress boots for ladies; they even sold "boot socks." I didn't realize you needed special socks to ride a horse. A trailer contained a wardrobe of out-fits for riders: trousers, coats, gloves, helmets and hats, again both Western and English.

I asked one vendor, "Why do you sell all this English stuff?"

"Because that's what most of the ladies want."

I thought riding horses was a "man thing," but, as I watched the show, I saw that many of the riders were women and girls, some almost as young as I.

Almost all the horses that weren't taking part in an event were wear-ing horse blankets. I wondered why when it was so hot. One of the handlers explained they used them to protect the horses from insect bites. It wasn't long after that I learned about horse flies and how painful their "bite" can be when one landed on my neck.

My favorite place was the smithy. Simon Parker had a building in the compound to house a smith, complete with furnace, bellows and several anvils. He hired a smith from a nearby county for the duration of the show. He fired up the furnace, unloaded a satchel of special tools, and was there to make horse shoes and other items needed by the contestants. I spent a lot of time watching him pound out shoes to order to fit specific horses.

His name was Reuben, and he was a big, strong man. He was tall, mighty, had huge hands and muscles. He didn't mind my hanging around asking questions and seemed to delight in describing each step. He said he had a son about my age. It was clear that he knew what he was doing and was proud of it. Once he let me pick up one of his hammers to strike a hot shoe. It was so heavy I had to use both hands to lift it and was never able to raise it high enough to make a decent blow.

One of the first poems I memorized in school was "The Village Blacksmith," and I saw Reuben as exactly the man Longfellow described:

> "Under a spreading chestnut-tree
> The village smithy stands;
> The smith, a mighty man is he,
> With large and sinewy hands;
> And the muscles of his brawny arms
> Are strong as iron bands."

I said, "Why don't you do the shoeing? It looks like other men do that."

"That's the special job for a man called a farrier. Here comes Grogan; he's a farrier and I'll let him tell you what he does. Maybe he'll show you."

Grogan was short, very thin, and had not one hair on his head. He led a dark brown horse with a white patch around one eye and was carrying a satchel with tools in it.

He checked the shoe that Reuben had made for size and held it to the horse's hoof. Grogan said, "That looks fine, Reuben."

He took out a tool that looked like a big set of pliers and used it to pull the nails out of one of the horse's hooves. Then he nailed on the new shoe. He gave the old one to Reuben who hung it on a nail. "Maybe I can use it again," he said.

"Doesn't that hurt the horse?" I said. "To nail into its foot that way?"

"No," Grogan said. "A horse's hoof is the same stuff as your fingernail. You cut your nails, and it doesn't hurt you. It's the same with a horse's hoof."

"What does a farrier do?"

He explained that a farrier is a specialist in horses' hooves, shoeing them, cleaning them, and taking care of any problems. "Imagine," he said, "you get a splinter in the bottom of your foot. It's painful to walk on it, and if you go without getting that splinter out, you can really mess up your leg limping on it. It's the same with a horse. I have to inspect their hooves to see if they have picked up a stone or a burr or something and take it out if they have. A horse is no better than the hoof it runs on. It's my job to keep their feet healthy."

Grogan said, "Would you like to help me lead Starfire back to the staging area?"

"Sure." But it scared me. I was not at all comfortable walking alongside that huge animal. I was proud of myself, and relieved, when I handed over the reins.

Thad, Stubby and I spent a lot of time at the food stalls, and soon most of the vendors knew our names and greeted us like we were old friends. I think they liked having us hang around; maybe it showed potential customers that something tasty was available with all those boys there. It takes a crowd to draw a crowd.

There were a number of food stalls: barbecue, sandwiches, soft drinks, popcorn, cotton candy, and plate lunches. Gramby's Women's Group from the Coldbrook Baptist Church had a stall to sell home baked goodies and canned goods. She said Simon Parker got a percentage of everything sold "to pay for the electricity." Gramby and I had been busy preparing cakes, cookies and candies. I learned a lot helping her and, the best part, got to lick the spoons and the pots and pans. She let me work the stall from time to time, but I spent most of a fun three days roaming the grounds, visiting with Reuben and Grogan, chatting with the other stall folks, watching the owners preparing their horses for the various events, and sitting in the bleachers watching the show.

When Gramby first told me that Simon Parker was having a horse show, I thought there would be racing. I found out, however, that it was all about showmanship, and there were judges to determine which horse and rider performed the best canter, jumps, trot, drills, or high step. I loved watching the jumping events, but my favorite became the sulkies. A sulky is a light, two-wheeled cart pulled by a single horse. The sulkies in the show were sleek and shiny, light weight and springy, the drivers decked out in fancy clothes, and the horse and driver fitted with the same colors. They were judged by their appearance, the control of the driver, and the ability of the horse to maintain its high stepping trot. If the horse broke its stride, it was out of the running. I watched the sulkies enter the ring, several at a time, and selected a favorite. I quickly became my own judge, cheering when "my" horse won a blue ribbon or complaining loudly when the judges didn't recognize its outstanding performance.

They did have a race. Men dressed as clowns ran a race on donkeys several times a day. They did the usual clown stuff: falling off their donkeys, straining to pull a stubborn donkey that wouldn't move, pulling down an opponent's pants to reveal colorful long johns, hitting each other with clubs made of pillows, getting into fights, and trading donkeys in the middle of the race. The clowns became a crowd favorite, and the stands were always full when they announced the Donkey Race.

Nancy Shorter, Chickie Frye, and Jimbo's sister Sarah sat under the bleachers and continuously sang "*Don't trade horses in the middle of a stream.*" Over and over they sang, and I could see it became annoying to the people in the bleachers watching the events. The girls sang and then laughed uproariously. Nobody else thought they were funny. The adults rolled their eyes and tried to see where the singing was coming from. But it didn't stop the girls. Every time a new event started, there was that song again.

On the last day of the show, Sam, one of the men who worked for Simon Parker, found me with Reuben and said Mr. Parker needed me. He didn't say why.

He took me to Simon Parker who said he wanted me to ride Fortune in the Parade of Ponies. Fortune was Junior's pony, and he was supposed to ride it, but he was sick. "I think Junior had too much cotton candy," Sam said.

I was to be the emergency substitute.

I admitted to Simon Parker that I had never ridden a pony. "Nothing to worry about," he said. All I had to do was sit on Junior's pony, hold the reins, and act like I was in complete control and happy. "Just smile," he said. He said Sam would lead Fortune around the ring two times, and that was all I had to do, just sit and smile. "Should I wave to the crowd?" I said. With a big grin on his face he said it would be fine.

As we lined up to enter the ring, I noticed that the three other riders, all young girls, were in special riding clothes. All I had on that day were dungarees and my brogans. I had on a presentable shirt, clean for a change, meant for my time in Gramby's stall selling blackstrap cookies. Somebody found a "cowboy" hat and put it on my head. Each of the girls dressed for the part. One was Dale Evans, another was in English riding habit, and the third was trying to look like the little girl in *Gone With the Wind*. Their ponies' gear and colors matched the girls' outfits.

I didn't know what the judges would look for, but, with those girls and their fancy outfits, I didn't expect to win anyway. I was nervous, but Sam told me for the fourth or fifth time not to worry. "I'll take care of everything."

I didn't have a chance.

Both times around the ring, when we got to the bleachers, Nancy, Chickie, and Sarah clapped and chanted, "Char-lee Payne! Char-lee Payne! Char-lee Payne!" I was totally embarrassed. I just tried to smile, and I even took my hat off and waved it at them the second time around. As we made the final turn, I saw Reuben and Grogan standing at the rail with Thad, Stubby and Gramby waving at me. They were cheering for me as I passed.

85

At the end of the event, the judges gathered and announced the results.

I won a blue ribbon.

So did the three girls.

It was the only blue ribbon I won in my entire life.

18

Naomi Parish

Naomi Parish was Aunt Bell's best friend in Coldbrook, except for Gramby, of course. She lived in a big house on Main Street on the north side of town "above the churches," as Gramby described it. It had four white columns in front, tall oak trees, a large formal side boxwood garden, and the only tennis court in Coldbrook. It was among the nicest homes in town.

When her husband died in an automobile accident several years before the war, she became a widow. But Naomi Parish was different from the other widows in Coldbrook.

In Coldbrook, when a woman became a widow, she became a "matron." They wear matron's clothes…black or gray dresses and low-heeled pumps…let their hair turn gray and pile it in a bun on top. Matrons spend their time in the company of other matrons. Married women tend to shy away from matrons and stop inviting them to social events in their homes. Could they be afraid that an attractive widow might steal away their husbands?

When my grandfather died, Gramby became a matron with all its Coldbrook traditions, dress, shoes, and hairdo.

Naomi Parish refused to fit the matron's role. She was different. Gramby said she was "a breath of fresh air." She cut and dyed her hair blonde. She invited married couples to her parties, and she had lots of them. She wore bright colored slacks around town; she was even seen playing tennis in shorts. The matronly class was scandalized, but Naomi didn't care. Aunt Bell loved her, and she was a regular part of our family get-togethers.

She drove around town in a Woodie convertible.

Naomi Parish was something of a force in Coldbrook. She was past President of the Coldbrook Garden Club. She started a book club and focused on books that were banned. She was among the first volunteers for local projects in town and at her church. During the war she had been Chairman of the local bond drive. The town received a letter from the Governor recognizing Coldbrook for the highest per capita participation of any town or city in Virginia. She sang in the choir at St. James Episcopal Church.

The first time I went with Gramby and Aunt Bell to her house, she asked me to call her Naomi. I protested, but she insisted. She was the first adult who made me call her by her first name. It was nice to be on a first name basis with such an interesting person.

With a smile and a wink, she said, "Charlie, can I fix you a glass of wine?"

I didn't know what to say and looked at Gramby. She had already balled her fist and put her thumb between her middle and ring finger—N.

She didn't need to make the O.

Then we all laughed together, and Naomi gave me a Coke.

On our way home Gramby said, "Naomi is good for Bell. She keeps her laughing."

For Christmas I gave Gramby a pair of slacks. Mama helped me pick them out. They were canary yellow.

19

Airplanes

Jamie Curry was one of the boys in my Sunday School class. We became good friends over the summer. He got me started building model airplanes.

He invited me to his house after church one Sunday so he could show me the models he talked about so much. Jamie had over a half dozen models in his room, some on string hanging from the ceiling as if "in flight." He displayed others on a shelf his father made. Most were military planes, biplanes from WWI and fighters from WW2.

"It's fun, and it's easy," he said, holding up a piece on which he was working.

I could see right away that building model airplanes was something I wanted to do.

He built his models with balsa wood and tissue paper. He explained they came in kits that contained plans and directions, balsa wood, tissue paper, dope, and decals needed to complete a model. He said he got kits at Harper's Hardware Store in Coldbrook, but their supply was limited. His grandfather bought kits for him at a model shop in Richmond and sent them to him when he couldn't find what he wanted at Harper's. "They are always on my Christmas and birthday lists," Jamie said. "Maybe, if we keep pestering Mr. Harper, he will get in more models,"

"How do you do it," I said, "and what do I need to get started?"

He was in the middle of building a P-38, a WW2 twin fuselage fighter. He showed me his tools and how he was building it. He explained putting together a model was pretty much how real airplanes were constructed over the years. "They built a frame of wood, added supports, added stringers, put the pieces together, and covered them with canvas. In time metal replaced the wood and canvas. We do the same, only with balsa and tissue paper."

It sounded easy, and it looked easy.

Jamie said, "You need a flat work place you can put pins and tacks into. You have to cut the stringers and parts; I use an Xacto knife and have a box of replacement blades. They get dull pretty quick, and the knife has to be sharp. And you will need scissors to cut the tissue paper. You use tacks and a lot of straight pins, so I get my Mom to keep me supplied with pins when she gets her sewing stuff. I buy extra glue and tissue paper, and you'll need a spray bottle to stretch the tissue paper on the model. You need a fine mist to moisten the tissue paper so it will dry evenly. Then you'll need brushes to paint on the dope."

I came home eager to get started and told Gramby about modeling, and how much fun it was and how easy it would be.

"Why don't we try one before we get too involved with them," she said.

"Jamie said we can get model airplane kits at Harper's Hardware Store right here in Coldbrook. The only other thing I will need is an Xacto knife to cut out the pieces."

"A knife? Where will you work? I don't want you cutting on the tops of my nice tables."

I hadn't thought about that.

"Maybe we could get a cork board like they have at church for the announcements. It would be big enough, and the pins would go in easily."

"Pins?"

"Yes, you have to hold the pieces together with straight pins while the glue is drying."

"Glue?"

"Yes, you need a special glue for model airplanes. It comes in a tube so you can squeeze it out right where you have to. I think it comes in the kit."

"I have enough straight pins in my sewing basket we can use. How much will all this cost? To get us started?"

I hadn't thought about that.

"Well, I think we ought to do a little investigating. Why don't we go to Harper's and see what Mr. Harper has in the store. He might even sell cork boards. And I'll ask at the church to see if they have an old one they would let us have."

We came home from Harper's and the church with a Piper Cub model kit and an Xacto knife with extra blades. Jamie had recommended a Piper Cub as the best starter kit. "It's the least complicated," he advised. The secretary at Gramby's church looked around in the closets and found an old cork board which she let us have. I was ready to start.

I tore open the box, removed its contents, smoothed out the plans, and tacked them to the board. I began cutting strips of balsa wood to fit the template for the frame and pin them down.

Gramby said, "Why don't we read the instructions first and lay out everything to see what we have and plan the steps we have to take in the right order."

I hadn't thought about that.

We laid out all the pieces and read the instructions.

"What's dope?" she said.

"It's a special kind of paint for model airplanes you put on the tissue paper covering. It makes it hard. You just brush it on."

"Brushes? I don't see any in the kit. Where can we get the small brushes we'll need?"

I hadn't thought about that.

"I'll ask Jamie where he gets his."

"What do we use to clean the brushes after we have painted the dope on the airplane?"

I hadn't thought about that either.

"Well, it might be a good idea for you to ask Jamie. We have time before we get to that part."

I was eager to get started, and I decided to tackle the frame parts first.

I cut strips of balsa to length, pinned them carefully over the template, and glued them together. When I put down the tube of glue, glue kept coming out on the plan.

Gramby said, "Why don't we try to use a pin in the opening to stop it up. Then we won't have glue all over, and we won't use it up so fast."

I hadn't thought about that.

I let the first part of the frame dry on the plans and tested it to see if it were ready. It seemed to take forever for the glue to dry. It looked great. When I lifted it up, the paper on the plan tore with it. I realized I had not covered the plan with wax paper. Jamie told me about needing to do that. In my haste to get on with the model, I forgot, and I ruined the template for the rest of the frame.

I decided that I would next build the tail assembly; it was small and looked easy to do. They stamped the forms for the tail on thin sheets of balsa, and all I had to do was carve them out with the Xacto knife. I discovered that cutting out those pieces required dexterity and patience, neither of which I had developed at that point. The first two split, and I tried to glue them back together, unsuccessfully. They were unusable. There was no way I could finish the Piper Cub.

I was dejected. I was at that awful stage where I wanted to give up building model airplanes on the one hand and I wanted to try another one on the other.

Gramby saved the day for me. She said, "Why don't we use the rest of the kit for practice. We can get experience in cutting out the pieces and gluing things." She even gave me an emery board that made a great tool for sanding the balsa pieces.

It took me three models and the rest of the summer before I got all the pieces attached on one. The wing was crooked and the tail off center, but it looked like an airplane. Gramby gave me an old perfume atomizer to spray the tissue, but I botched painting the dope. I was too embarrassed to show it to Jamie.

Several of the boys talked about an air show taking place at an airfield a few miles outside Coldbrook. Turnbull Field was nothing more than a long grassy field, a windsock, and a gas tank. It was home to several crop dusters who flew over the area farms and tobacco fields. Sam Turnbull, the owner, was a crop duster and an antique plane enthusiast. He had a hanger (actually a big barn) with several vintage WWI era airplanes he liked to roll out and show people.

Jamie told me they would also have a model airplane show at the same time. He said, "We really ought not to miss out on such an important event. Everybody will be there, and we can see what other people are building. They'll be flying real models. We can learn a lot. I entered my P-38 in the competition."

I told Gramby about the air show and that Jamie and I wanted to go, and that I would learn a lot about modeling, and that it would really be fun. She smiled and said, "Why don't I call Mrs. Curry and maybe we can all go together."

On the day of the show, Gramby drove me, Jamie, and his mother to Turnbull Field. It was a beautiful day with only a few clouds high in the sky.

I liked seeing the old planes and hearing about them from Jamie, who seemed to know a lot. Mr. Turnbull was patient with us boys and explained the details of each plane, what its mission was, and how it performed in the war.

They set up the model show on one side of the hangar, and a crowd of people, young and old, was milling about. Jamie and I ran over and looked for his entry to see if he had won a prize. He hadn't won one of the prizes, but he got an honorable mention in the balsa category. I know it disappointed him, but I said I *really* liked his P-38, and it was *really* well done, and it was *really* neat he got an honorable mention when the other entries were by older boys, and I *really* wished I could make one that good.

I'm not sure that made him feel better, but we moved on to look at the other models. I must admit that I was disappointed as well. I had expected to see a lot of planes like the ones I was trying to make: balsa and tissue. However, most were hardwood models with cloth exteriors, clearly out of my league. They impressed me, and I could see the workmanship that went into building them, but I realized it would be a long time before I could reach that level. In a way it made me more determined to be a great modeler.

They announced that the model demonstration was about to start, and the four of us went over to the edge of the field to watch. Mr. Turnbull had arranged for a representative from a model company to demonstrate something new to Coldbrook, a radio-controlled airplane. For most, it was our first opportunity to see what was then a new capability, new at least for Coldbrook: to fly a model airplane remotely using radio signals.

The model representative made a brief talk that explained how it worked and what he wanted us to see. He then started up his airplane, which had a small gasoline engine, started it down the field, and when it reached a certain speed, lifted it off the ground into flight. We yelled and clapped when it got airborne. He commanded the plane to circle the field, make a low-level pass, bank left and right, climb to a high altitude, go into a slow dive, and then level off and land. All the commands were sent from a box he had placed on a table. The box had a control stick he moved, just like a pilot might, to cause the model to maneuver where he wanted.

He refilled the fuel tank each time for two additional runs. When he finished the last flight, he was given a big cheer, and we crowded around him with questions. He politely tried to answer all. He said you had to be a trained pilot to fly the model because the same skills were needed. Jamie and I were excited and talked about how much we would like to fly one of those models one day even if it meant we had to go to flight training.

One of the crop dusters, a man called Slim, offered to take people up for a flight for $3.00. I asked Gramby if I could go although I was a little scared but tried not to show it. Jamie sounded brave and matter of fact as if he had flown many times. It would be the first time for both of us. Gramby and Mrs. Curry talked it over, said "yes," and gave Slim the money.

As Slim, Jamie and I walked out to the plane, I asked him where he learned to fly and how long he had been flying. He laughed and said, "I joined the Army Air Corps when I was seventeen. They needed transport pilots; I volunteered; went to flight training; and then qualified in DC-3's. I flew missions out of India for three years during the war." Once I saw a movie about our pilots flying "over the hump" from India into China. I was pretty impressed.

He crammed Jamie and me side by side into the open back seat of his plane and strapped us in. He said, "If you get sick, do it over the side. I don't want to clean up a mess inside the plane."

I hadn't thought about that.

We took off with the two of us holding on tightly to the sides of the plane. Once airborne, we were in another world. I couldn't have imagined how exciting it was and how beautiful everything looked below us. To look down and see farms and tobacco fields with their straight rows was unbelievable. Slim flew over Coldbrook, and I recognized the center of town and the Courthouse and railroad tracks and the ball field. Boys were on the field looking up at us. I touched Slim on the shoulder and pointed to the ball field and motioned for him to go around for another pass.

Slim banked around, dropped altitude, and flew low over the ball field. The boys started waving at us, and I could see they were yelling. One of them, I think it was Harley, tried to throw a ball at us. We waved back at them.

I loved every minute of that flight and was disappointed when Slim banked and turned for the field. The landing was bumpy, but we settled down and taxied to the edge of the field near Gramby and Mrs. Curry. Neither of us got sick.

I decided right then I would be a pilot someday and have my own plane and take kids up for a flight. It was a dream that didn't come true, but I have spent the rest of my life fascinated by airplanes.

When we got home, Gramby said, "Next time, why don't the two of us go up with Slim."

Every kid should have a Gramby like that.

When I went home at the end of the summer, I took the cork board, my Xacto knife, my brushes, and the perfume atomizer. I also took back a solid determination to build a Spitfire fighter. Gramby sent me the kit for my birthday.

It was never finished. I forgot the wax paper.

20

Mrs. Haymore's Porch

We were playing catch in the shade of Thad and Stubby's yard when Mrs. Haymore came out on the porch with a bowl in her hands.

"You boys think you can fill this bowl with blackberries?"

Thad said, "The birds haven't left very many, but we'll try."

We headed out to the pasture and picked the berries we could reach along the edge of the briar patch. We could see more, but they were in the interior. None of us wanted to go in there no matter how many berries were there.

"I've got an idea," I said. "Let's use our bats to hold back the stalks and make an opening, and I'll try to reach the ones inside without getting a thorn in my arm."

It worked, at least enough times to fill the bowl to overflowing. We took it back to Mrs. Haymore who was sitting on the porch waiting for us. She only had to clean up a few bloody briar scratches.

"Good work," she said. "I'm going to make a cobbler. You boys think you would like some?"

Three voices in chorus, "Yes, Ma'am."

We went back to playing catch, and after about an hour, she came out on the porch with a tray of bowls with blackberry cobbler. Thad and Stubby's little sisters joined us.

"I thought you might like a little ice cream on the cobbler."

Another chorus, "Yes, Ma'am."

Mrs. Haymore knew how to make a great cobbler: fresh berries picked by hungry boys, served warm on the porch right out of the oven, and topped with vanilla ice cream.

Later in the summer I rode down to Thad and Stubby's as usual for some baseball. When I got there, they said they couldn't play just then. "We have to help Mom pick tomatoes," Thad announced. "They're ripe now, and Mom's in a canning mood. You want to help?"

"Sure," and I went with them to their tomato patch. They showed me how to tell which tomatoes were ripe enough for picking and stressed the importance of placing them carefully in the baskets without bruising them. It wasn't hard work, but it was hot work. There was no shade, and as we picked, I got thirsty and could feel pain in my legs and back from bending over.

We filled three baskets and carried them to Mrs. Haymore on the porch. She said, "You are doing a great job, and I appreciate it. You boys think you would like some lemonade?"

The usual chorus, "Yes, Ma'am."

We sat in the shade of the porch and cooled off. She brought us another round of lemonade.

We filled eight half bushel baskets with tomatoes before Mrs. Haymore said we had picked enough for the day. "I'll be a few days getting all these canned up, so you boys go play baseball. I will need you to pick some more in a few days." She said, "Thanks, Charlie, I hope you will come back and help again."

"Yes, Ma'am."

To the pasture we went, but we didn't play long. We were tired and went back to the porch and asked Mrs. Haymore if we could have more lemonade.

Tomato season at the Haymores turned out to be a fun time. Picking tomatoes became a regular pastime for a few weeks, and it was always accompanied by something good to eat and drink on Mrs. Haymore's porch.

Many afternoons, after hitting and pitching and shagging flies, hot and dirty and sweaty, we left the pasture. We picked ripe tomatoes growing in the hot summer sun and rested on Mrs. Haymore's porch in the shade. With a big shaker of salt alongside, we made quite a mess. Sprinkle some salt on a hot tomato, take a big slurpy bite, wipe your mouth on your arm, shake on more salt, another bite, and another wipe. Mrs. Haymore would sometimes contribute a gallon jug of cold buttermilk or Mason jars full of lemonade which helped wash down our feast. Then we went to the pump to wash up. There was an occasional tomato fight, and we got pretty messy. We went down to the bottom of the hill and jumped in Stony Creek.

Sitting on Mrs. Haymore's porch was also a time for boy small talk. National League or American League? Yankees or Red Sox? Truman or Dewey? Oldsmobile, Ford or Chevy? What is Junior High going to be like? Joe DiMaggio or Ted Williams? Why do they have five churches in Coldbrook when they all teach the same things about Jesus? Jackie Robinson? Army or Navy? Why are girls so different? Chocolate, vanilla or strawberry?

We never agreed. It didn't matter. We were still buddies.

21

Arthur Willard

Arthur Willard delivered mail to Gramby every morning, Monday through Saturday. I thought he was an amazing man. How could he drive a left-hand drive, stick shift Chevrolet, while sitting on the right side to put the mail in the boxes? How could he manipulate the clutch, the brake pedal, the gas pedal, and steer at the same time? He was a wizard.

Mama and Daddy sent me a postcard every week while I was in Coldbrook. Gramby must have taught Daddy about post cards. They wrote how much they missed me, and how much they loved me, and how they hoped I was having a good time. I loved those postcards. They usually arrived on Tuesdays, and I made a practice of going out to meet Mr. Willard at 8:45 each morning. You could count on his being on time. That's how I got to know Mr. Arthur Willard, Tuesday mornings waiting for my postcard.

Gramby told me that when Mr. Willard wasn't delivering the mail, he was an expert woodworker. She pointed out the bookshelves he built on either side of her living room fireplace. She said he designed and constructed her bed, a chest of drawers, and two side tables out of solid cherry for her bedroom. She said his fine furniture was in great demand in Coldbrook and he could make a good living doing just that. But Arthur Willard liked delivering the mail; he made furniture and other wood items for the joy he received in doing it.

"Arthur Willard is a master craftsman. Few people can claim that title."

"What does that mean?"

"Master craftsmen are men and women who create beautiful things with their hands. They have special God-given talents, have the highest standards, are wonderfully creative, and produce one-of-a-kind works of art. They work for years to develop their skills, to make their objects better and better. Their passion in life is to create things that give them joy. I think that must be how God felt when he made us."

"Are they just wood workers?"

"No. They can be potters, sculptors, glass makers, weavers, or quilters, just to name a few. Many who create objects in wrought iron are master craftsmen; remember your friend Reuben from the horse show. There are wonderful artisans in this world. Arthur Willard is one of those rare people."

The next time I met Mr. Willard at the mailbox, I told him I liked what he had made for Gramby. I asked him if I could see how he made things like that.

"That would be fine," he said. "Have your grandmother bring you to my workshop in the afternoon. I usually finish my mail route by two or two-thirty."

His workshop was a large, one room building, neat and clean. He welcomed us and said he liked to keep his workspace clean and his tools organized. "That way," he said, "I don't have to go hunting around for something and waste time." He showed me his electric saws, drills, sanders, a lathe, and other pieces of equipment and explained how each one was used in making furniture. He said he would be happy to have me come back and watch him while he was working on his next project…"if you'll be careful."

I was delighted with the invitation and spent many afternoons at his workshop, watching and learning.

"How did you learn to make these things?"

"My grandfather taught me how to make furniture and use tools. He didn't have all these electric tools. He made a lot of his own, and many were run by foot pedals." He opened a cabinet and showed me his collection of antique tools. "My grandfather made most of these."

Several times he let me use one of the drills or do sanding. He let me help clean up. "Maybe I can make a real cabinet maker out of you one of these days," he said. "I think you just might have a knack for it."

He couldn't have said anything that would have made me happier.

We talked a lot about baseball. He was a Washington Senators fan, and he talked about the years when they were a good team and even won the World Series. He said his favorite player of all time was the pitcher Walter Johnson. He was sad the Senators had dropped to the bottom of the league with the Browns and Athletics. "They just can't keep up anymore with the Yankees, Red Sox and Indians."

A few weeks before I returned home, Mr. Willard said he had a surprise for me. He opened one of his cabinets and took out a baseball bat. "I turned this on my lathe for you out of a piece of ash that I had; it's the same wood they use for Louisville Sluggers. I burned your initials, CHP, in the right place so you will know how to hold the bat and not break it."

I was speechless. I held the bat in my hand and took a few practice swings. I even remembered to be careful not to hit anything in his workshop. I finally mumbled out my thanks. He gave me a small bottle of oil and told me to rub the bat down with the oil every week or so.

When I got to Gramby's, I asked her for a postcard and wrote him a thank you note.

My visits in Mr. Willard's workshop gave me a lifelong appreciation for fine craftsmanship. I look for and visit craft fairs, try to meet and support craftsmen, see them at their work, and even buy a few items. He taught me the value of keeping tools neat. He said, "Know where things belong, put them there when you're finished using them, and you won't have to search for them when you need them."

That is a lesson I have taken to heart, not only with tools, but with other aspects of my life…kitchenware, clothes, books and personal records. It saved me a lot of time and frustration. I learned it's a whole lot easier to find a sock in the sock drawer than lost under the bed.

I still have Mr. Willard's bat. I keep it in my closet. From time to time I take it out, take a few practice swings, and oil it down.

22

In *This* Family

We were quiet on the porch at tweenlight. I asked Gramby, "Where did I come from?"

Gramby hesitated for some time, smiled, and said, "Haven't you talked with your Dad about that?"

"Oh, I know all about that stuff. No, I'm talking about family, about being a Hester. You always talk about what we do in *this* family and the Hesters. You were a Hester; where did they come from? What's so special about the Hester part of our family?"

"We aren't any more special than anyone else...but no worse. Anytime you start thinking you are better than someone else is when you get into trouble. Just wait for the letdown. I'm not talking about running or batting or things like that. Sure, someone may be faster than you, or smarter, but that doesn't mean they are a better person than you are. That's really what counts in life...what kind of person you are."

"But you are always saying 'in *this* family' or something about 'my people' or 'our people.'"

"I know I do, but that's just a term I use for family. My Papa used that term for family. My grandfather did as well. It's the way we talk. I'm proud of my people because they handed down a set of values over the generations that stand for integrity and honesty and caring for others. I saw those characteristics in my parents and their parents, and they talked about the same things being handed down from their ancestors. It has helped me set the standards for my life, what I try to live by."

"What do you mean by integrity?"

"It certainly has a lot to do about honesty and keeping your word. The best definition is that it means doing what is right even though it may cost you something."

"What do you mean...it may cost you something?"

"Well, say we go uptown for lunch at Mrs. Parker's Diner and we have sandwiches, drinks, and dessert. When she brings us the bill, she forgets to charge us for the ice cream. What are your choices of what to do?"

"You can walk out with free ice cream or you can tell her and pay for it."

"And probably no one would ever know. What's the right thing to do?"

"Tell her and pay for it."

"I'm glad to hear you say that."

"Well, it's the right thing to do, but it costs us for the ice cream."

I thought about that awhile and said, "I can think of another example. When I'm playing baseball, there are times when a player might be called out, but I know I juggled the ball. Wouldn't the right thing be to tell the truth and let the player be safe? My team mates may not like it, but that's the right thing to do. The point is you would want the other boys to do the same thing if you were called out."

"I'm glad to see you have a good understanding of what's right and what's wrong...and why. Most people do know what's right and wrong, but not everyone is willing to pay that cost. Sometimes it's a little thing like calling a man safe, but sometimes it's a lot. You don't have to be an adult to know what's right. I think you know right now."

Gramby was quiet for a while and said, "There is something inside you called a conscience. I know you know it's there. Your conscience is what tells you when you do something right and when you do something wrong. And if you do something wrong, it is your conscience that will tell you, and keep nagging you about it. Sometimes it makes it hard to live with yourself and makes you wish you could make things right...to give back something you've taken, or to apologize for a bad remark about someone, or say that you cheated."

"I understand, but I still want to know where I came from. What do you know about our family? about our people? Where did the Hesters come from?"

"Our family isn't just Hesters. You are a combination of Payne and Thompson, half and half. Your Dad is a combination of Payne and Hester. I am a combination of Hester and Springer. You have two parents, four grandparents, eight great-grandparents, sixteen great-great-grandparents, and so on. You have over a thousand great grandparents in just ten generations or so, and that's over a thousand separate families all coming together in you."

It was my first lesson in genealogy.

"Wow, and there were more before that. But then why do you always talk about being a Hester?"

"It's because I grew up being a Hester. Until I was married to your grandfather, I was always a Hester. I knew my mother was a Springer, and I knew her parents and all my Springer cousins whom I loved, and my aunts and uncles, but I was still a Hester. That's true of most people; they claim the name they were born with as primary. I'm sure you think of yourself as a Payne. It's part of who you are."

"Yes, you're right. If you ask me, I'm a Payne."

"For every generation of Hesters in our family tree, there was another family. Each of your grandmothers back up the line brought a new family to our tree, so all their ancestors are part of our history as well. The Hesters came to Virginia from England, but we also have Scotch, Irish, Welsh, German, Dutch, and probably some more on our family tree. There certainly could be even more families."

"Did the Hester men marry women from all those countries? How did they meet them all?"

"No, that's not how it happened. Some generations ago a Hester man married the daughter of a family with Scotch and Irish ancestry. Then all his descendants had blood from English, Scotch and Irish nationalities. The same happened when a Hester ancestor married a woman who had German and Dutch ancestry. You have all that history because you are a descendant of everyone in the chain to some degree or another. I don't know that much about your mother's people. You could have a lot of other countries represented from her ancestors."

"How long have the Hesters been in America?"

"Our people have been in America for a long time, except for the native Indians, about as long as anybody."

"How long ago was that?"

"The first ones came to Virginia in 1619. They were a young English doctor and his wife. Thaddeus Hester was from a well-to-do landed family from Derbyshire, but he had to leave England because he made the social error of falling in love and marrying a Quaker girl. Church of England England was not particularly hospitable to Quakers in 1619. Our ancestor and his new wife settled upriver on the south bank of the James River at a place called Parsons' Hundred. They had two sons there."

"And we're descended from one of them?"

"Yes, let me tell you the rest of that story. There was an Indian uprising in Virginia in 1643, and it was led by Pocahontas' brother. You know who she was. They attacked the Hester cabin. During the battle they hid the boys, one under a washtub and the other in the potato hole."

"What's a potato hole?"

"It's a place dug in the ground where they stored potatoes. It was covered up during the battle."

"Were any of them killed?"

"The attack was pushed back but not before an arrow killed Thaddeus Hester at the cabin door. A traveling schoolteacher, who happened to be there giving lessons to the two boys, shot and killed four of the attackers. When two Indians came down the chimney, the quiet Quaker mother poured boiling water on one and ran the other through with a hot meat spit.

"Wow! That sounds scary."

"The two boys went on to become important people in early colonial Virginia. One of our ancestors was among the first to attend William and Mary after it was founded in 1693. Our people have always placed high importance on education, for both men and women. Our Hester ancestors include a governor, two members of Congress, a Bishop, two county sheriffs, and," she said with a smile, "my cousin, a reserve pitcher on the Chicago Black Sox baseball team. If a family has been in Virginia a long time, we're probably related."

"You have a cousin who was on the Black Sox? A relative of mine?"

"Yes, my cousin Walton, but he didn't play much."

"Was he banned?"

"No, Walton wasn't one of the starters and wasn't good enough to be involved in that mess."

"Wait till I tell Thad and Stubby."

She said, "Whenever the Hester people gather for reunions, weddings and funerals, we ask each other, 'Are you a washtub Hester or a potato hole Hester?'"

"What am I?"

"You are a potato hole Hester."

23

Revival

There were three big events in Coldbrook every summer: the carnival, Simon Parker's Horse Show, and the weeklong Revival at Coldbrook Christian Church. Coldbrook Christian Church up on Main Street was one of the smaller churches in town; most Coldbrook folks were Methodists, Baptists, Presbyterians, or Episcopalians. Everyone was protestant; the colored folks in and around town went to the Bethel AME Zion Church. There was not a single Catholic or Jewish family in town.

Although Coldbrook Christian had a relatively small congregation, during their annual revival week it was always crowded with people from the other churches. Revival week at Coldbrook Christian Church became a town tradition, and the church fathers made every effort to bring in exciting speakers each year. My baseball buddies were talking about it for weeks and many declared their intentions of attending. Lance told me his family were members of Coldbrook Christian, and he gave me a personal invitation to attend. "You have to go to the revival. Everybody does. It's one of the best weeks of the summer. I even wear a clean shirt every night."

For weeks there was a big sign in front of the church advertising the event. Gramby said most of her friends made sure they knew the dates of the revival each year before they made summer plans.

"Gramby, everyone's talking about the revival. Can we go?"

"If you would like to, we certainly can. I wouldn't miss it for the world."

The Reverend Billy Ray Walton from Valdosta, Georgia led that summer's revival. Gramby said Reverend Billy Ray, as he asked everyone to call him, was well known on the revival circuit. He led the revival in Coldbrook several years before and was quite popular. All Coldbrook was excited about his return. He was a powerful speaker, preaching love and forgiveness to repentant sinners. Reverend Billy Ray was a showman, raising or lowering his voice dramatically, pacing along the stage, and pointing to the crowd for approval and an "amen" for the high points of his sermons.

Reverend Billy Ray also played the trumpet with the music during the service, making sure he played a solo interlude or flourish after each verse of the songs. The music made the evening special. Shorty and Lance sat with us, and Nancy Shorter, Chickie Frye and Sarah joined us. For once, the girls didn't give us trouble. All the kids talked about Reverend Billy Ray's trumpet playing and how it raised the roof of the church and how it lifted the spirits of the congregation and how it was the highlight of the whole week.

They announced that there would be special awards for those with perfect attendance. Nancy Shorter told us she wanted to be there every night to get that special award. Most of the kids agreed with her. Gramby asked me if I wanted to go again.

I said, "Of course, it's fun." I'm not sure that's what she would like for me to have said, but we had dinner early and set off for the church. I liked to watch Reverend Billy Ray preach, and I especially liked the music and his trumpet. Joining in the singing was my favorite part. It was also fun to be with the other kids. We sat together each night.

Two special events happened at every meeting. One was the passing of the plate to allow everyone to join in the "mission of the church to spread the Gospel." While the music played and another trumpet piece was heard, the plates were passed. I put in a little something each night. Then Reverend Billy Ray thanked the people for their generosity and always found a reason with an appropriate Scripture verse to pass the plates one more time...and play another song on his trumpet. Two nights during the week the plates were passed yet a third time. I never understood whether the "mission of the church" had to do with Coldbrook Christian Church or with the good Reverend Billy Ray.

At the end of the sermon each night Reverend Billy Ray made what Gramby told me was the "Altar Call."

With emotion and passion Reverend Billy Ray prayed aloud that "these good people of Coldbrook, young and old" would find it within their hearts to repent of their sins and come forth to ask for forgiveness. "Come to the Cross and give your life to Jesus."

While the music played softly in the background, Reverend Billy Ray sent up mighty prayers in his most powerful voice. The first night only a few people went up. Heads turned to see who was going forth. I heard mumbling. Were they wondering what sins were being forgiven?

Each night more people went forward. It looked like a lot of folks in Coldbrook needed forgiveness. Reverend Billy Ray laid a hand on each one and raised the other to heaven, thanking God for "saving this person from a life of damnation." Shorty and Lance and several other kids were among those who went forward to receive his blessing. Nancy Shorter was one.

I was not. Every night when I went to bed, I thought about what Reverend Billy Ray had said in his sermon. I knew I too needed a lot of forgiveness. I was tempted to go forward but got cold feet at the last minute. I didn't want any of my friends to ask me what I needed forgiveness for. Gramby said nothing about it, and I was glad she didn't encourage me to go forward.

My friend Stubby had the "misfortune" of being born on the 24th of July, which just fell on the last day of the revival. It was the tradition in his family to make a big celebration of the children's birthdays. His parents invited a large crowd of kids to a birthday party for Stubby on that very Saturday evening. His Dad rented three ponies for pony rides at the party and arranged for a fireworks display in the cow pasture. Several suggested that they move the party to another day or at least to a different hour so the kids could go to the revival and get their perfect attendance awards.

Mr. Haymore said no. He said his son's birthday was more important, and that this was his family's tradition, and he would not change the party. All of us chose to go to the party.

The only exception was Nancy Shorter. She told Stubby's mother she couldn't come to the party because she had made a commitment to attend the revival. She did send Stubby a large package of BB's as her present.

Nancy Shorter got her perfect attendance award...a lapel pin...and my everlasting respect.

24

Peach Ice Cream

Postmaster Sydney Waterson's nephew had a good peach crop that summer, and Mr. Waterson, good friend that he was, made sure that Gramby got a bushel of his nephew's peaches. I learned that a bushel can hold a lot of peaches. We ate peaches whole, and we cut them up on cereal for breakfast. Gramby made peach pies and peach cobbler. I loved them.

A few days after the peaches arrived, Gramby said, "Why don't we make some peach ice cream. I'll get it ready and mix it up and we'll let you turn the crank."

"Crank? What does a crank have to do with ice cream?"

"Yes, you have to turn the crank to make the ice cream. I'll show you how it works. You'll like it. It's fun."

Gramby brought out the ice cream maker. It consisted of a wooden tub, a round metal canister, a thick metal bar the crank fit into, and a contraption that looked like paddles joined together. "This is the dasher," she said.

We peeled a dozen peaches, removed the pits, and cut them into small pieces. Gramby put half into a bowl and said, "While I mix up the cream, why don't we mash these." She gave me the potato masher and showed me how to start. When I finished mashing, she put all the peaches into the cream mixture, stirred everything together, and poured it into the canister. It was about an inch shy of filling it. "We don't want to fill the can to the top; we have to leave enough room for the ice cream to expand as it freezes or it would overflow," she said.

"How does this thing work?"

"This kind of ice cream maker has been around for a long time. My grandmother had one, so they must be about a hundred years old. She gave me the recipe and showed me how to make it work. I've been eating ice cream for about as long as I can remember. The canister with the cream rotates when you turn the crank," she said. "We'll put ice and rock salt around the can to get it super cold."

"Why salt?"

"The salt lowers the temperature around the can and the subzero water then pulls the heat out of the cream as the ice melts. The cream freezes inside at the edge of the canister. We will have to replenish the ice and salt from time to time. I'll show you when. Why don't we start. You carry the bucket."

We took the maker outside under the apple tree. She put the canister in the bucket, inserted the dasher and put the top on the can, clamped down the top piece, and connected the crank.

"We'll be out here a long time so it's best we be in the shade. Now the ice." Together we filled the bucket, mixing in rock salt as we did.

"This is getting complicated."

"Just wait. Time to turn that crank."

"Why do we have to turn the crank?"

"When you rotate the canister with the crank, the dasher scrapes the ice cream off the inside and lets more cream get to the edge. Eventually, all the cream freezes and then we have a can of ice cream."

"How long do I have to turn it?" I was already getting tired.

"About an hour."

"That's forever."

"Well, you can trade arms ever so often. Just make sure you always turn it in the same direction. I know it's a long time, but I'll keep you supplied with water to drink. You will think it is worth the effort when you taste the ice cream."

As the canister turned, the ice melted and salt water dripped out of a hole in the side of the bucket.

"Why the hole?"

"We don't want salt water to rise enough to get into the cannister; the hole is there to let the water out before it can. Just keep going on that crank."

As I cranked, Gramby kept adding salt and ice from time to time.

"It's getting harder to turn. Is it finished? How can you tell if it's ready?" I was getting tired and a bit annoyed.

"When we can see cream coming out of the canister, it means its full of ice cream. It will also be hard to turn then."

I thought I must have been turning that crank for hours. Both arms were aching. I switched hands several times, but I finally saw white cream leaking out of the canister.

"Now?"

"I think so. Let's take it inside as fast as we can."

She dismantled the crank and top piece and carefully lifted out the can with the dasher still in it. We moved quickly to the kitchen. She opened the canister, and behold! I saw beautiful ice cream!

Gramby lifted out the dasher and put it in a large bowl. It was covered with ice cream. She spooned off some and returned it to the canister and replaced the top. The dasher was still covered with lots of ice cream.

"In *this* family when someone turns the crank on the ice cream maker, he gets to clean the dasher." She gave me a spoon and said, "Go to it."

Every kid should have a Gramby like that.

We put the cannister back in the bucket and packed more ice around it to keep it cold.

I cleaned that dasher of the best ice cream I've ever eaten. That first taste of homemade peach ice cream, cranked personally by me, made it my favorite for life. We ate homemade peach ice cream for dessert every night until it ran out.

We made several different kinds of ice cream that summer: chocolate, strawberry, raspberry, and plain old vanilla, but none equaled the peach. I told Thad and Stubby how much fun it was to make homemade ice cream and wouldn't they like to come over the next time and take turns cranking. My arms needed the help.

When I got home, I talked Mama into giving Daddy an ice cream maker for his birthday. "We can get the recipe from Gramby, and I will teach him how to turn that crank."

25

Handin' Leaves

"We're going up to see Zeet and Della. Why don't we bring our pj's and toothbrush and some changes of clothes," Gramby said. "We'll spend two or three nights; I'm going to help Della with her canning. Zeet's pulling tobacco, so take plenty of old clothes; he'll want you to help."

I wanted to tell Gramby it meant I would miss a big game the boys were planning, but I decided it was better not to complain. "When are we leaving?" I tried to act excited. I didn't know a lot about Uncle Zeet and Aunt Della. I saw them at the occasional family gathering but never talked with them much except when Mama nudged me to say hello. I did remember that Aunt Della brought the best pies.

Uncle Zeet was my grandfather Lane Loudermilk Payne's youngest brother by almost twenty years. He and Aunt Della lived in what I thought was a house from another century. They had no electricity, no indoor plumbing, no phone, no heat, except for a fire place...and *no radio!* It *was* from another century. How could they live like that? They used kerosene lamps and candles at night, and Aunt Della did all her cooking on a cast iron wood burning stove. However she did it, her food was delicious.

Gramby told me she had been born in a farm house like that. "Imagine, in one lifetime, I've come from a house with no bathroom to a world with automobiles, telephones, electricity, and airplanes."

As soon as we did our hello's and hugs, Aunt Della told me to put on my old clothes so I could help "handin' leaves." I didn't know what "handin' leaves" meant, but Aunt Della said, "They'll show you. It's easy." I changed, and she led me out to the tobacco field and Uncle Zeet. He welcomed me with a big smile and introduced me around. It was tobacco pullin' and tobacco curin' time on the old Payne farm.

With his boys now away in the Marines, he hired a local family to help bring in the tobacco crop, and so I met JimmyJohn Johnson, who was in the field pulling leaves. He and Uncle Zeet went plant to plant and pulled the leaves that were ready from the bottom up. The leaves were loaded onto a wheelbarrow and carried by JimmyJohn's son Jasper to a spot on the edge of the field in the shade of a huge hickory tree. Uncle Zeet placed wide planks on saw horses to make a trestle table. That became my place of work.

JimmyJohn's wife Oholibama had the job of tying the leaves onto sticks that would go into Uncle Zeet's tobacco barn for curing. I joined two of her daughters, Emerald and Ruby, in handing her the leaves. The girls told me their oldest sister Pearl was home with baby Beryl. They explained, "We're all named after the jewels in the Bible."

They showed me how to pick up three leaves from the table, push them together so the stem ends were flush, and hand them to Oholibama. In almost no time I became an expert at "handin' leaves."

Oholibama was a magician. I still can't figure out how she could take a handful of tobacco leaves, attach them to a square stick, and tie them down securely...all in one motion as fast as we could hand them to her. She always seemed to have her hand out waiting for the next set of leaves. I would have needed four hands--one for the leaves, one for the stick, and two for the string. Oholibama was a huge woman and, except for scolding Emerald, Ruby and me to "hurry up with them leaves," she was either smiling or singing.

Nobody knows the trouble I've seen

Nobody knows but Jesus

Nobody knows the trouble I've seen

Glory Hallelujah!

And everyone joined in, *"Glory Hallelujah!"* Soon I was joining right in with them. Then Oholibama would start a new song.

Every time I feel the Spirit

Movin' in my heart,

I will pray.

In two days of handin' leaves I learned *Go Down, Moses, Swing Low, Sweet Chariot, Joshua Fit the Battle of Jericho, Down by the River Side*, and many more. And she always added, *"Glory Hallelujah!"* to every song.

Every leaf I touched left a deposit of black tobacco tar. Soon black tobacco tar painted any uncovered spot on my skin. Where I touched my face or scratched a spot, there was tar. And then my clothes were covered. After we quit for the day, it took Gramby and Aunt Della an hour to clean me up at the pump behind the kitchen. Aunt Della heated water in a cast iron pot, and with her homemade soap and a hard bristle brush they removed the tar. I will never forget that brush; it felt like steel fingers.

"Where's the bathroom?" I asked Aunt Della. She laughed and said, "You'll have to use the outhouse," and pointed to a little shack on the edge of the back lawn. I never used a privy; in fact, that was the first time I actually saw one. I could just go behind a tree and pee, but I had a more urgent requirement and had to face the terrible dangers of the outhouse. I knew it would smell. I knew it would be dark. I knew that just behind the seat it would have at least one hornet's nest and probably a yellow jacket's nest. Hornets and yellow jackets don't like to be bothered, and they attack when you invade their space. I knew there would be cobwebs and big hairy spiders. I knew there would be rats, big ones. I knew I would get long, sharp, painful splinters in my behind. And I knew that down in that hole there were big, angry, hostile snakes just waiting to bite my private parts.

I hesitated, looked at Gramby, and looked at the outhouse. Uncle Zeet put his hand on my shoulder and said, "It's okay."

And it was.

I was starving after my day of handin' leaves and was ready to eat. Aunt Della put out a wonderful dinner, and I went back for seconds and thirds, especially for the raspberry pie. Aunt Della said, "We picked those berries just this afternoon."

On the last night Gramby and I were there, Uncle Zeet said, "I've got to keep that fire going in the tobacco barn. I'll be there all night." He looked at me and said, "You wanna help?" I looked at Gramby, she nodded, and I said, "Sure!" We carried a couple of old blankets, two Mason jars of water... and a piece of pie for me... and headed off to the tobacco barn.

When we got there, Uncle Zeet said, "We need to go back to the woodpile and bring more wood. I'll fill the wheel barrow and you can take an arm load. We may have to come back in the night, but I've got a good stack already at the barn."

My armload of wood was heavy, but we added to the stack, laid out our blankets, and settled in for a night at the tobacco barn.

Uncle Zeet said, "My father's great grandfather built this barn. That would be your great, great, great grandfather. More than a hundred years ago."

"That's a lot of greats."

"He had to cut down the trees, drag them to this site, and shape them into these square logs. I think they are all hickory logs; there are a lot of hickory trees around here. Then he had to cut these notches just right to make the barn fit together. He only had what we would call old timey tools...a few different kinds of axes, a chisel, a level, and a plumb line. And the logs were heavy; I suspect that he had neighbors who helped him raise this barn. And look at those big stones that make the foundation. I don't know how he learned to do this work, but he made a sound barn, and it's lasted over a hundred years. He must have had some strong mules to do all that hauling."

Uncle Zeet went around the barn and pointed out the fine work that went into building it.

"He must have been a great carpenter to do all this."

"Yes, he was, and most of the people in his generation had to do the same, to build their own homes, barns, and other buildings. The best thing is that we can still use the barn today, after all this time."

It was one of those especially clear nights without a speck of cloud cover. As the darkness overtook us, we settled down on our blankets, looking up at an incredible night sky. Uncle Zeet knew everything about the stars, and we could see millions. He pointed out the big and little dippers, the North star, Orion, and Venus and the Milky Way. He explained constellations...that they weren't really stars in a bunch but just what they seemed to be when you looked at them. I had no idea what light years were, but he tried to explain it. It was a night filled with shooting stars, and he explained that they were meteors burning up in the atmosphere.

It was my first lesson in astronomy.

He told me stories of growing up on the farm with Grandfather Payne and Meemie and what good people they were and how much he missed them. He said they named him after President Zachary Taylor because Grandfather Payne's grandfather had gone off to fight with General Taylor in Mexico.

"I didn't know that. I thought your name was Zeet."

"Well, that's my nickname. When I was little, they first started calling me 'ZT' because Zachary Taylor was too long. Then it just got shortened to Zeet."

"You should be proud of your name, after a President and all."

"I am."

Uncle Zeet told me how his great grandfather had marched in Washington, D. C. with a special Honor Guard of veterans on inauguration day, and how President Taylor invited them for "punch" at the White House after the parade. "I still have the cap he wore in that parade."

"I'd like to see it sometime."

We talked baseball. He liked the Cardinals and Stan Musial. He said his father gave him a ball and glove when he was about my age, but he was never able to play much. The boys who lived around him all had chores on their farms. It was hard to get enough of them together at one time to play a game. "I still have that glove."

He said, "If you and Elizabeth come back, bring your glove and we'll throw the ball around."

"I will. Could you teach me how to throw a curve ball?"

"Not really, but you could ask Jasper. JimmyJohn tells me that Jasper is a good pitcher on his school team."

Uncle Zeet got up several times, poking at the fire, throwing on more logs, and peering inside the barn making sure all was okay. He looked down at me and said, "You hungry?"

"I sure am."

He went across the dirt road to the corn patch, pulled off two ears of corn, came back, and threw them into the fire. He poked them occasionally with a stick, pushed them out of the coals, and when they had cooled enough, he pulled back the husks and gave one to me. "Be careful; it's hot." It was also delicious; I never had an ear of corn that tasted better.

I finally fell asleep and was surprised when I woke up with the sunrise and I had slept all night. The fire was still going strong, but I hadn't heard Uncle Zeet during the night. Aunt Della came down to tend the fire while Uncle Zeet went to the house to grab a few hours sleep before going back to the field. She brought some warm biscuits and freshly made raspberry jam.

When Uncle Zeet woke up, Gramby and I said our thanks and goodbyes. I ran over to the hickory tree to say goodbye to JimmyJohn and

Oholibama and Jasper and Emerald and Ruby. Oholibama was singing *"Gimme that Old Time Religion,"* and I joined in for one last time.

I think I can still hand leaves with the best of them.

Glory Hallelujah!

26

Girls' Choice

It surprised me to get an invitation to Mary Jane Clark's birthday party. She was in my Sunday School class, but we never became close friends, never saying much or paying attention to each other.

I asked Gramby, "What can I get her? I don't know her that well, so I don't know what she would like. It must be a big party if I am included."

"Why don't we go up to Mrs. Tomlin's Ladies Apparel Shop and see what we might find for Mary Jane. It can't be something too personal or too expensive, but let's get something nice. I'm sure Mrs. Tomlin can help us find a present she will like."

We spent about an hour at the Dress Shop, and Gramby recommended that we settle on a colorful scarf. Mrs. Tomlin offered to wrap it as a gift, and we stopped by Doc Gravely's Drug Store to buy a birthday card to go with it.

Jimbo's sister Sarah knew Mary Jane had invited me and told me it would be a very special party. She said everybody was supposed to dress up, and the girls would wear their best party dresses. "You should wear a tie; I'm sure the other boys will. You'll be glad you did."

"Who else is going?"

"Nancy Shorter and Chickie Frye and two other girls I don't think you know. Sally Ann Chambers and Betsy Matthews. They're good friends of Mary Jane's."

"I've heard some of the boys talk about them, and I think I've seen them around town. Do you know what other boys she invited?"

It turned out that only six boys were invited, including Jamie and Tommy. I didn't know the other ones. Why was I included in such a small number? Six girls and six boys. I didn't know what to expect, but I was excited to be a part. To be on the invitation list as a newcomer to Coldbrook, I had expected a large number of kids. It looked like this would be a rather small party.

I checked with Jamie and Tommy and found out that Sarah had told them to wear ties too.

The night of the party I ironed my pants and shirt, and Gramby helped me with the tie. I had yet to master the art of the necktie knot.

"You look terrific," she said. "a lot like your Dad."

I walked up to Mary Jane's house near the library on Main Street and was greeted by Mr. and Mrs. Clark. They ushered me into the living room to meet the others. I said my hello's and gave Mary Jane my present. The girls were dressed in their finest. The boys all had on ties. Sarah rushed over and said, with a big smile on her face, "See, I told you all the boys would wear ties. You look nice."

Mary Jane pointed me toward the dining room for refreshments. Her parents had prepared fried chicken drum sticks, macaroni and cheese, and fries. The cake ceremony and ice cream followed the food. Mary Jane blew out the twelve candles in one blow as we sang "Happy Birthday."

The boys stood on one side of the table; the girls stood on the other.

Mary Jane then invited everyone back into the living room to watch her open her presents. I was nervous about that, and mine just happened to be the last one she opened. I felt better when she said, "Thank you so much, Charlie. I love the scarf. I saw it at Tomlin's and have wanted it for a long time. It was really nice of you to get it for me."

I secretly thanked Gramby.

With the last present opened, Mary Jane said, "Now it's time to party. Everybody out to the sun porch. Let's dance!"

Dance? I didn't know how to dance.

Mary Jane put a record on, and the girls started to dance with each other. They knew what they were doing. The boys just stood and watched. I was getting more nervous every minute.

When the first song ended, Mary Jane announced, "Girls' choice!"

Each girl went directly to a boy; Chickie Frye came to me.

Flash! Now it was clear. Mary Jane picked the girls she wanted at the party, and the girls "suggested" which boys to invite. It had all been neatly arranged. But still: why me?

Chickie stood in front of me, held out her arms, and said, "Charlie, you want to dance?"

"I've never danced before," I confessed. "I don't know how. I don't know what to do."

"It's easy. Just put that hand on my waist and hold this one and just move your feet to keep time to the music. You just have to relax."

I was so embarrassed. I looked around at the others. The girls were giggling and trying to get the other boys to dance. They looked just as anxious as I was.

Except for Jamie. He was with Nancy Shorter, and they were already dancing. He told me later that his mom had given him a few lessons because she liked to dance and wanted him to know how.

Chickie said, "This is a great song by Tommy Dorsey; come on, let's try it."

I took her hand, held her waist, and she put her arm on my shoulder. I did my best, and soon I relaxed and did find I could move with the beat of the music.

I was dancing!

There I was dancing with Chickie Frye in my arms. Chickie Frye from my Sunday School class. Chickie Frye who pestered us at the movies. Chickie Frye who heckled me at Coldbrook Field. Chickie Frye who embarrassed me at the horse show. We danced one more song together. "Glenn Miller," she said.

Then Mary Jane announced, "Boys' choice."

I panicked. I think the other boys were just as confused as I. Whom to select? Why?

Out of desperation I chose Mary Jane. Gramby told me before the party I should pay special attention to the birthday girl. I tried to do what Chickie taught me. I wasn't so bad and enjoyed dancing with Mary Jane.

Mary Jane thanked me for the dance and said, "I didn't know you could dance so well."

I said my thanks and felt good about myself.

She then announced that it was time for a jitterbug. Again I was lost. I had no idea how to jitterbug. Not one boy stepped up to try, even Jamie.

The girls knew what to do and danced with each other. *"How would I ever learn to do that?"* I thought. The girls were moving fast, shuffling their feet in a rhythm I couldn't catch. The boys just watched.

As the party progressed and I gained confidence, I decided to dance with all the girls at least once. It was fun dancing with Sally Ann. She acted like I knew what I was doing, and we talked and laughed a lot. Most of the couples danced in silence, not knowing what to say. Sally Ann seemed to be a nice girl, and I was glad to get to know her. Sarah talked through the whole record and didn't give me a chance to open my mouth. Betsy accepted my invitation with a nod of her head and never said a word the entire song. She was stiff and danced in jerky movements. She seemed very nervous and uncomfortable. Had I scared her for some reason?

My last dance was with Nancy Shorter. I guess I was doing all right; she gave me another compliment on my dancing ability.

Chickie asked me to dance one more time, and we started just as Mr. and Mrs. Clark came in to say thanks to all of us for helping to make Mary Jane's birthday so special. It was an obvious message that the party was over.

When I got home, Gramby and I stayed up late as I told her about the party, who was there, what we ate, about dancing with each of the girls, and how much fun it was.

"I'm proud of you, Charles, for being such a gentleman. It was the right and proper thing for you to dance with all the girls."

"And you were right, Gramby, about the scarf. Mary Jane said she had been wanting that scarf for a long time and was thrilled that I gave it to her."

It was my first boy-girl party. It was my first dance...the first of many to follow in my life.

Years later my wife taught me how to jitterbug, and it's now our favorite.

27

Homer Benson

Homer Benson ran a dairy farm on the highway south of town. He raised cows and had two prized bulls he kept in separate pastures. Gramby said every year those bulls produced enough calves that, besides his dairy business, he made a handsome income from selling his excess calves. Every Saturday, Mr. Benson delivered a pound of butter and a gallon jug of buttermilk to our house. A lot of families in Coldbrook had their milk and butter delivered by Mr. Benson every week.

Mr. Benson built a railroad alongside a flat portion of the road by his farm. It consisted of an engine and two open passenger cars. The engine looked a lot like a tractor on a rail chassis. There was a shed at the end of the track to house everything. The track was only several hundred yards long, maybe the length of two or three football fields.

On Sunday afternoons when the weather was nice, Mr. Benson started up his railroad and let the local kids come for a ride. The railroad went nowhere; it just went back and forth. I went once with Thad, Stubby and Barry Lee Jamison, but after a couple of such short rides, I lost interest. Nancy Shorter, Chickie Frye and Sarah came often and made pests of themselves, singing *I've Been Working on the Railroad* over and over. Mr. Benson didn't seem to mind, but everyone else did.

I asked Gramby, "Why did he spend all that money to build a railroad that doesn't come from anywhere and isn't going anywhere? That's a funny place to build a railroad."

"Some people in town call it 'Homer's Folly' behind his back. Homer has always loved trains. Having his own railroad makes him happy…and it makes the children happy. I guess that's reason enough."

Years later, driving to Coldbrook to see Gramby, I passed the spot along the highway where Mr. Benson's railroad had been. I looked for the flat area he had carved out of the side of a hill to make a place for it, but I would not have recognized it if I had not known about it. The area was overgrown with trees and bushes, and they were covered with kudzu.

"Homer's Folly" was no more.

28

Abraham Sparks

One morning Gramby said, "Why don't you come with me to pick up one of my cane-bottom chairs."

She said there was only one man she trusted to weave the bottom, Abraham Sparks. As we drove, she told me his story. "He is the best at caning in the area. Everybody uses old Abraham. He is probably the oldest person I know in Coldbrook," she said. "He loves to tell how he was born a slave before the Civil War and was freed by Abraham Lincoln when he was a small boy. Most of the slaves on the farm left the area as soon as they could, but he, his mother, and the elderly ones stayed. Over the years he did odd jobs and learned how to weave cane backs and bottoms from his grandfather. He is a special artisan."

"How old is he?"

"Nobody knows. I don't think even he knows for sure, but I would guess he is around ninety. Now he doesn't see that well and can barely walk, but he still does beautiful caning. He suffers from gout."

"What's gout?"

"It's a very painful form of arthritis. Imagine getting sharp pieces of glass in between the bones in your ankle or knee or wrist. I'm told that it is unbelievably painful. I can understand why Abraham has such a hard time walking."

"How do you know so much about him?"

"When Abraham was young, he worked for a long time for your great grandfather Payne. Then he worked on and off for us when your grandfather and I were newlyweds. He loved to talk with me about his history, and I have tried to keep up with his family."

"How does he get along? Is there that much caning work?"

"He lives with his granddaughter Minnie and a bunch of children out of town. That's where we are going. Minnie works for Mrs. Overton uptown as a house maid. Most of the time she walks two miles to town and back, but sometimes, when it's bad weather, Mr. Overton will drive her home."

"Why don't they pick her up. That's a long way."

"You don't know Mrs. Overton."

We turned up a narrow, potholed dirt road and pulled into a red clay clearing. There wasn't a blade of grass or other green thing showing. There was a tar paper covered house that looked a lot like Uncle Zeet's tobacco barn. I thought Uncle Zeet's barn was much nicer. The house had a door, one window, and a slanting front porch. It looked like the whole thing was about to fall down. That house has always been what I see in my mind when I hear the word "shack." Next to the house was a hand water pump, and at the edge of the clearing was an outhouse.

An old white-haired man was sitting in a rocking chair on the porch fanning himself.

Gramby and I walked up to the porch, and she said, "Abraham, I've come for my chair. Minnie called and said it was ready. This is my grandson, Charles, who is staying with me this summer."

"Hello, Miz 'liz'beth. That's a fine lookin' boy. Mr. Charles, you takin' good care of yo' grandma?"

"I'm doing my best," I said. "Pleased to meet you."

Five children were standing by the side of the house watching us. They were dirty, skinny, barefoot, and holding on to each other as if they were afraid of us. They just stood there, silent, in ragged clothes, and stared at us. A mangy looking black and brown dog, of unrecognizable parentage, rocked back and forth next to the children and growled at us.

"The chair is ready," Abraham said. "Chastine, fetch that chair for Miz 'liz'beth." The oldest of the children went into the house and came out with Gramby's chair. "I'm teaching Chastine to cane," he said. "She's gonna be good." There was a big smile on his face.

Gramby examined the chair and said, "That looks fine, Abraham, mighty fine. I will give you a little more than we agreed on because you did such a special job for me."

"Whatever you think is fair, Miz 'liz'beth. I sure am grateful."

She added, "and there's an extra dollar for something for the children." It was the first time I saw them smile.

"That's mighty nice of you," he said. "What do you say to Miz 'liz'beth?"

"Thank you, Ma'am," they said in a sing-song chorus.

Gramby reached in and pulled out several bags from the car. "I also brought you some of my canned butter beans and some grapes that Charles and I picked just yesterday. Sadie Whiteside sends a dozen eggs and a mess of turnip greens. Here are two pairs of shoes I hope the children can use."

Chastine took everything into the house. The other children followed close behind.

"Thank you, Miz 'liz'beth. You are always so nice to us," Abraham said. "And tell Miz Sadie I'm grateful."

I put the chair in the back seat. As we were leaving, Gramby said, "Abraham, are you getting your medicine?"

"The county lady comes by every other week with my medicine, but sometimes she forgets. She must be busy with other folks."

"Well, I'll speak to her when I see her. Abraham, you make sure those children get to school this fall. You tell Minnie to call me if they need anything."

"I will, Miz 'li'beth; I'll tell her."

We said our goodbyes and headed home.

I must have been quiet for a long time when Gramby said, "You okay?"

"Gramby, why are they so poor?"

She too was silent for a few moments as we drove along.

"Abraham and his family have been poor all their lives. He is a good man, but he has led a tough life. He never learned to read and can only sign his name. Most of his family dispersed after they were freed, but he and his mama stayed and worked on the farm."

"Why didn't they move on?"

"Because they had no place to go and no way to go. They could never dig themselves out of being poor. They're barely educated. Many of his people never went to school at all, and too many that did go dropped out to go to work to make some money...so they could eat. Most of the boys left as soon as they got big enough to look for work. There isn't much for them here in Coldbrook. It's only the old ones who seem to come back...to finish out their lives."

"Hasn"t there been anyone to help them?"

"Well, Janie Willet, the county agent, is supposed to visit them to take Abraham his medicine and food and clothing for the children. But then she gets busy, and Abraham and his family, like too many colored folks, fall to the bottom of the list."

We drove in silence. Then Gramby said, "I ask for clothes at church from families whose children have outgrown theirs. But, there's not enough, and sometimes I get busy with my own life and just don't think about Abraham and his family."

She was silent yet again and then said, "I'm not proud of that."

There was another period of silence as we traveled. She said, "The only colored people white folks know in Coldbrook are ones that work for them, and they have no idea what it is like where colored folks like Abraham live. The real problem is that the white folks don't care and the colored folks don't complain, at least not out loud. Eventually one of the other has to change."

As I picked up the cane-bottom chair from the back seat, I said, as much to myself as to Gramby, "They all gotta change...and soon."

When we got inside, she said, "I think I will call Janie Willet and see if she'll let me take Abraham his medicine. And we can take him a bottle of aspirin; maybe it will help the pain in his feet."

We walked back to the kitchen. I grabbed a blackstrap cookie from the tin. She said, "Why don't we make some of that peanut butter candy to take to those children?"

When Chastine was in her teens, she worked for Gramby several days a week, helping her with house cleaning and the ironing. Gramby pushed and pushed her to finish high school. She helped Chastine get into one of the state teacher colleges, and when she graduated, Chastine came back to Coldbrook to teach.

At the age of 94, Gramby stood in the Bethel AME Zion Church, tears streaming down her face and with her arm about Chastine when they announced that Chastine Sparks was the newly elected Mayor of Coldbrook, VA.

Every kid should have a Gramby like that.

29

Nadine Pruitt

N adine Pruitt lived in one of Aunt Bell's apartments at the Hotel Grover. Most people considered her an outsider even though she had lived in Coldbrook almost thirty-five years. I did recognize that she "talked different;" I could tell she wasn't a native. Gramby said she was from "out west in Arizona someplace" and came to Coldbrook when she married a local man.

Between Gramby, Aunt Bell and Nadine herself, I learned a lot about her.

People considered her husband, Ernie Pruitt, the best baseball player to come out of Coldbrook High School. My barber Hargrove still talked about his feats on the diamond. He left town to much fanfare to play professional baseball in 1914 for the Tucson Old Pueblos in the Class D Rio Grande Association. He is the only man in Coldbrook history to play professionally. He was batting above .300, played second base, and became a local favorite of Tucson baseball fans.

He was a quiet young man who stayed away from after-game partying with the other Tucson players. Instead, if games were over early enough, he showered and dressed for Sunday evening services at a local Baptist Church. That's where he met Nadine. At the end of May they were married at home plate between games of a double header. One of the biggest crowds in Old Pueblos history witnessed the blessed event. A week later the Rio Grande Association folded, and the teams disbanded. Ernie and Nadine had just enough money left to buy tickets for the train ride to Coldbrook. Ernie's elderly parents welcomed their new daughter-in-law into the family. Gramby said she never seemed to be able to make close friends with any of the local young women her age. They may have been jealous of "that outsider" stealing away one of the most eligible of local bachelors.

When America entered WWI, Ernie volunteered and, after training, shipped out with the Marines to France. He was killed in action at Belleau Woods, and his body was never recovered. By then Nadine had no family left in Arizona, so she stayed in Coldbrook. She worked at several jobs around town and eventually received a war widow's pension. When Ernie's parents died, she was left alone.

She grew up in a small town at the edge of the desert in western Arizona. When she was 12 her parents were killed in a mining explosion, and she went to live with her only living relative, great Aunt Mabel who lived in Tucson. That's how she came to meet Ernie Pruitt.

Nadine seemed to enjoy spending time with me when I stopped in at Aunt Bell's. I enjoyed hearing her tell stories about being in the desert, and I kept asking her more questions. I always pictured a desert as nothing but a blazing hot gigantic sand pile. She told me about desert plants, and flowers, and birds, and animals…and snakes…all the creatures that lived there. She talked about how it cooled at night and how it was so clear the stars came right down to earth. She told me she still missed the desert and would love to go back sometime, but for now, "I'm staying in Coldbrook." I told her I would love to go with her if she does.

Nadine had the unusual habit of attending all five of the churches in Coldbrook, a different one each Sunday. She sang soprano in every choir in town, but you could never tell where she would show up until choir practice that week. At first people didn't understand and criticized her for what they thought was a lack of commitment. In time they accepted that it was just Nadine, just her way of trying to get along with everyone.

She was the only woman in Coldbrook who wore jeans in public. Nadine was in Naomi Parish's book club.

30

Hesters

We came home after a dinner with Naomi Parrish and Aunt Bell and sat on the porch. We talked awhile and sang a few of the songs Gramby taught me. It grew quiet after we stopped singing, and it began to get dark. I asked Gramby how she knew so much about our Hester people over such a long time.

"Bibles."

"Bibles?"

"Yes, bibles, and handed down family stories. My grandfather Hester had a family bible in which they recorded births, deaths and marriages for at least five generations. When I was born and when I was married are listed in that bible. I have it now and will show it to you. You might like to read that information about our people. I put your Dad's name in it, and when he married your Mom, and when you and your sisters were born."

"I would really like to see that."

"My grandfather inherited his great-great-grandfather's bible. It included five more Hester generations, so we have good information going way back to the first Hesters in Virginia. My sister is keeping that old bible for the family; I made a copy of the information which I can show you as well."

I loved to hear Gramby tell stories about her "people," as she always spoke of her family and ancestors. She liked to tell how her people came from England to Virginia "before those Mayflower folks." She said they had fought the Indians, the French, the British (twice), the Mexicans, the Yankees, the Spanish and the Germans (twice). She didn't want to talk about her youngest son, Uncle Joseph, who was killed in Normandy during the war. I understood I shouldn't ask.

One of my favorite stories was about a Hester at the time of the Revolution who was a friend to two men who became U. S. Presidents.

"Lucius Hester was the brother of my great-great-great-great-grandfather, Morton James Hester. When the revolution started, Lucius left William and Mary College and joined the American army. He was an Aide-de-Camp to General Washington from beginning to end, from Boston to the victory at Yorktown. He crossed the Delaware at Valley Forge with Washington."

"He was close friends with Alexander Hamilton and James Monroe who both served on Washington's staff. At the time of the battle of Yorktown, the Hester family owned land just outside the battlefield, and the family made it available to the American forces. Particularly important were the wells for fresh water. After the victory, Lucius watched the British soldiers lay down their guns on Hester land and march away. He said it was the proudest moment of his life. His friendship with Monroe was such that the future President named his second daughter Maria Hester Monroe. Lucius later served ten years in the Virginia legislature."

"My cousin Daniel was a hero in the Spanish-American War."

"When was that?"

"In 1898, just before the turn of the century. Daniel was in the Navy for almost twenty years before the war started."

"What did he do?"

"The Admiral asked for volunteers to go with a Naval Officer named Hobson to sink an old American ship at the entrance to a harbor in Cuba, and my cousin was one of eight who volunteered."

"Why did the Navy want to sink one of our own ships?"

"The purpose was to bottle up the Spanish fleet in the harbor, and they did it. Other than Teddy Roosevelt, there was probably no one in the country more popular than Lieutenant Hobson after that feat. He won the Congressional Medal of Honor, the highest medal you can get."

"And what about our cousin?"

"The men were taken prisoner by the Spanish but were exchanged a month later, and every one of them received the Medal of Honor."

"So a Medal of Honor hero is one of our people?"

"Yes. Sadly, Daniel died as soon as he returned to the states. He picked up a disease in Cuba, probably malaria. None of us had the chance to congratulate him."

"There was another important military man in my life, my grand-father Charles Morton Hester. That's where you got your name, Charles. He joined the Confederate Army of Virginia when Virginia left the Union. He was an artillery man and fought from Bull Run to Gettysburg to Fredericksburg to Appomattox. He told us he had a horse shot out from under him three times and saw countless men cut down around him. In all those years Grandaddy never had a scratch except for losing two fingers in the Wilderness Battle.

"How did he lose two fingers?"

"He told us his battery scored a direct hit on a Union ammunitions dump. When it blew up, Grandaddy raised his arms and jumped up and down in his excitement. A random Union gunshot hit his upraised hand and left him without the last two fingers on his right hand."

"Did it keep him from doing things?"

"Not really. He had to learn new ways with that hand. Most important was he still had his thumb so he could grab things and write. He could plow and hoe and rake, and he could still tickle his grandchildren. He played the banjo and, when he came home from the war, had to teach himself all over how to pick it with his thumb and two fingers. We loved to hear him play and begged him to bring it out when we were together. I think everyone thought he was the best banjo picker in the county."

"Grandaddy said he asked the Lord why He had spared him when so many others were killed or badly wounded. He was convinced that the Lord wanted him to come home, marry my grandmother, and have a son. That son was my Papa, and that's how I'm here, and that's how you are here. We're part of an unbroken chain of people going back and back."

"If the chain had been broken, we wouldn't be here."

"That's right. I can see you understand where we came from."

31

Chickie Frye

On the first weekend I was in Coldbrook, Gramby said, "Why don't we go to church tomorrow. Lay out some of your nice clothes and be sure to take a bath tonight." Every Sunday that summer Gramby and I went to the Coldbrook Baptist Church for services and Sunday School.

There were four girls in my Sunday School class, and I became the fifth boy. The only ones I knew at first were Frankie and J.B., baseball kids I already met. Jamie Curry became one of my best friends that summer as he introduced me to the fun of making model airplanes. I didn't pay much attention to the girls, but one of them, Chickie Frye, later played a memorable role in my life.

Mrs. Mabel Watson was a delightful teacher and one of my favorite people in Coldbrook. She was smart and made us laugh; she made going to Sunday School fun. On my first Sunday she welcomed me into the group with a smile and a big hug and made me feel one of them right from the beginning. Mrs. Watson knew the Bible from cover to cover, and I thought she could quote the whole book. No matter what the subject might be, she always came up with an apt passage to make her point, complete with book, chapter, and verse.

As a retired fifth grade teacher, she knew how to get everyone in the class involved. She also knew how to keep the boys from pulling Mary Jane Clark's pigtails.

We spent the summer learning about some great people of the Bible.

Mrs. Watson taught us that there was a common theme that carried through in these stories. Her basic lesson was that God used the heroes of the Bible to do mighty things, but that each one was flawed. She pointed out that Jacob stole his brother's birthright and created dissention among his sons by showing favoritism to Joseph and Benjamin. Joseph showed off before his brothers. Samson was selfish and impulsive; how could he be so stupid to give Delilah his secret after she betrayed him three times? David failed to raise his children wisely and committed adultery and murder. Solomon got caught up in riches and wives and failed to prepare his son to rule after his death. Peter was in frequent conflict with Jesus and denied him three times.

The lesson was simple and easy to understand. Despite their flaws, she said God used these heroes for His purposes. None was perfect; that can be said for only Jesus. Just the same, He can use each of us, even though we are imperfect. I am grateful to Mrs. Watson for helping me understand that lifelong lesson. I have tried to remember that when I have done the wrong things in my life.

Chickie Frye was one of the girls in the class. Gramby told me when Charlotte Simpson Frye was a toddler, her father called her "my little Chickadee." As she grew older, that was shortened to "Chickie." Gramby said, "Horace and Marlene Frye are fine people, and Chickie is a nice young girl."

I don't think I have ever heard a better nickname for anybody; it ranks right up there with "Muddy" Waters and "Dusty" Rhodes as all-time greats.

I saw a lot of Chickie over the summer. She always seemed to be about town with Nancy Shorter and Jimbo's sister Sarah. The three of them showed up at the ball field to heckle the boys and embarrassed me at Simon Parker's horse show. They were pests in the movies. Chickie taught me to dance at Mary Jane Clark's birthday party. I never paid that much attention to any of them. That changed when Chickie Frye tried to kiss me after Sunday School.

I was standing outside the door of Sunday School when she called "Charlie, wait."

Without saying a word, she walked up to me, put her hand behind my neck, and pulled my face to hers. I jerked away as she closed her eyes and puckered. She missed. Neither one of us said anything. She looked me in the eye and then walked away.

I was surprised.

I was also surprised that I rather liked the idea of being kissed by Chickie Frye.

It was my first experience of thinking of girls as something other than, well, just girls.

I liked it, and there began for me a new outlook on life. There were more things in life to be interested in than baseball and reading about world travelers...and that now included girls.

There also began a new game in my life, the game of young romance, and a game it was, with rules, and winners, and losers. Most of my later experiences with the "game" led me to believe it was a game for losers. Fortunately, I have had the one victory that matters.

This is the game: In one of the grand mysteries of life, Player A (Chickie Frye) likes Player B (me), but Player A doesn't know if Player B shares that sentiment. Then enters Player C (Nancy Shorter), who is the "impartial" Go-between enlisted by Player A to search out the feelings of Player B. Player A would dare not confront Player B with the direct question, "Do you like me?" That would place Player A in the earth-ending risk of being humiliated by a negative answer. Player C can ask the question and relay the answer at an appropriate time. Player C may provide just a hint that Player A likes Player B to get the game going. The single rule for

Player B is to avoid answering one way or the other at all costs. Thus the game can continue.

It is also important to understand that the word "like," in this game, has a much different meaning than liking baseball or liking black-eyed peas or liking The Lone Ranger. In the game of young romance, "like" takes on the glow of "love," but it's not quite there, except, perhaps, in the mind of either the liker, the liked, or both.

The few weeks that remained of my stay in Coldbrook saw the two of us playing another game in which we tried our best to avoid each other while trying to see each other. We couldn't avoid Sunday School, and there was no mention of the "almost kissed" event. Neither of us brought it up. I would not have minded if she had.

A carnival came to Coldbrook each summer, and it was a time when we kids roamed the grounds as a big group. Chickie and Nancy were standing just in front of me in the line for the Tilt-a-Whirl. At the last second, Nancy stepped aside; the operator hollered, "Next," and pushed Chickie and me into the seat and put down the bar. Nancy was beaming and giggling.

We sat as far apart as possible, but when the ride started, gravity forced us together. Chickie grabbed my arm with both hands and held on for the entire ride. When the ride stopped, she looked at me as if I had just saved her life. She whispered, "Thank you," got up, and disappeared into the crowd. It made me feel I was the most important person in the world. Nancy looked at me like she had won the best prize at the carnival...and just giggled.

On my last Sunday in Coldbrook, Chickie Frye came up after Sunday School, grabbed both of my hands, and kissed me on the cheek. She said, "Good-bye, Charlie. I'll miss you."

I gave her a hug and promised I would write her a postcard when I got home.

I never did.

I have no idea whatever happened to Chickie Frye, but I am grateful to her for being the first to play the game. Could she be considered my first like?

32

Hargrove

The only barber shop in Coldbrook was on Main Street in the center of town across from the Courthouse next to Gravely's Drug Store. It was owned and operated by a tall, white haired black man named Hargrove. Whether that was his first name or last none of my friends knew. He was known universally in town as "Hargrove."

After I had been at Gramby's a few weeks, she said, "Why don't we get you a haircut."

Uptown we went, and I was introduced to Hargrove, the town barber. About every two weeks thereafter she sent me uptown to Hargove's Barber Shop for a trim. Except for the few boys I knew whose mothers cut their hair at home, almost every Coldbrook male of haircutting age, old or young, was a regular customer at Hargrove's.

Gramby said, "Most of the leading citizens grew up going to Hargrove's from their first haircut on. He is a town institution."

Over the summer I looked forward to my visits with Hargrove. He joked with me, teasing me about my being so short, about my muscles (or lack thereof), and being a "city boy." He told great stories about his people, about the good citizens of Coldbrook and its history, and about my grandfather, Lane Loudermilk Payne. He told me that my grandfather was one of his favorite customers, and he added, "and I cut your Daddy's hair too. He used to fidget a lot; I had to hold him down sometimes to get him to sit still."

I think he was trying to tell me something...to sit still.

Hargove told me he remembered my Uncle Joseph, an Army Lieutenant who died in France during the war. "Your Uncle Joseph was one of the nicest young men in Coldbrook. I gave him his first haircut and cut his hair the whole time until he went away to school. I don't think I ever knew any young man who was politer than your Uncle Joseph. Everybody liked him. And he was a good pitcher, won a lot of games for the high school."

"I really didn't know him. I wasn't old enough when he went into the Army to remember much about him. About the only thing I remember is tumbling with him down the bank in back of Gramby's house just before he left for the Army. I didn't know he was a good baseball player."

"When we got the news about France, I was surely sad. I went to see your grandma to tell her what a fine young man he was and I was sorry she had lost him. It was such a loss for her, and for all of us in Coldbrook. It seems like it's the nicest ones who didn't come back from that war."

"Thank you for telling me about him. Gramby doesn't talk about him because I know it makes her sad, so I don't ask. I'm glad to get to know a little more about him."

"You just be as nice as he was, and you'll do fine in this world."

On my first trip to Hargove's he didn't ask me how I wanted my hair cut; he just started. When he finished cutting, he wiped a straight razor several times on a wide leather strap and then covered the edges in back and over my ears with hot lather. Then he shaved those areas clean and followed with a warm towel to clean up the lather. He cut a sharp line. A vigorous scalp massage followed that. He finished the job by rubbing in a pungent hair tonic. I never felt he was rushing me so he could get to the next customer. He made me feel important.

The fragrance of that hair tonic stayed on me for days.

Most boys and men in town smelled the same. I had noticed a peculiar smell in the air almost everywhere I went in Coldbrook. After my first haircut, I recognized that it was pure Hargrove hair tonic. Most of us boys not only smelled the same but looked the same, at least as far as our hair style was concerned. It was vintage Hargrove.

It is the style I prefer to this day.

On my last haircut, Hargrove sent me home with a bottle of his hair tonic. "You keep using this," he said, "and you'll catch all of those young ladies in the big city."

When I got home, I gave it to Daddy. I told him I thought he might remember it.

33

The Thimble

We were getting everything ready for a birthday dinner that Gramby was giving for Aunt Bell. Miss Pat, Naomi, Judge Law, and the Watersons were coming. We were going to have Gramby's meatloaf and mashed potatoes, black eyed peas, fresh-cut tomatoes and onions, and her wonderful brown sugar pie. I was glad to learn that Aunt Bell's favorites were the same as mine.

I was getting dressed when a button came off my shirt. I asked Gramby if she would sew it back on. She said she would have to wait until the next day. "Just put on another shirt till then."

The next morning, she said, "Why don't we learn how to sew on a button. Get your shirt."

She said we had to remove the old threads first and took a tiny pair of very sharp pointed scissors and cut away the remaining threads. "It has to be completely free of the old thread to make it easier to push through the new."

She then showed me how to moisten the end of the thread to make it easier to put through the eye of the needle. She let me try it several times before I felt confident doing it. "You can probably do it more easily than I because you have better eyesight," she said.

The next step was tying the knot. She moistened her fingers and showed me how she rolled the ends of the thread together to make a knot. It looked like magic, but she made a secure knot. Again, it took me a number of tries before I succeeded in making a usable knot. She cut the knot off and had me try again and again until I was able to do it consistently.

She showed me the button and said, "Imagine the button is a clock face and the four holes represent twelve, three, six, and nine o'clock. You can sew in a cross pattern: twelve to six and three to nine, or parallel: twelve to three and six to nine."

It made sense.

"Why don't we do a cross. Now when you start, come up from the bottom through twelve and go down through six and then up through nine and down through three."

I tried to follow her directions but had problems getting the needle to go through the cloth. "It hurts my finger when I try to push the needle up. Even the blunt end is too sharp."

"That's why we use this," and she handed me what looked like a miniature metal cup.

"This is a thimble. Probably thousands of years ago somebody had the same problem you are having and invented the thimble. You put it on your finger and can then use it to push the needle through without putting a hole in your finger."

"Which finger do you use?"

"I use my middle finger so I don't have to take it off to pull the thread through. It saves time."

After a few pulls and pushes, I began to get the hang of it. "That thimble really helps."

She watched me closely and when I had made about six turns around the clock, she said, "Now let me show you how to tie it off so it won't unravel."

When we finished, I buttoned my shirt and headed off to Thad and Stubby's.

I must have fixed five or six buttons over the summer. I had a new skill and kept adding new ones. Gramby taught me how to repair a hem in my trousers and how to darn socks. She had something that looked like a wooden egg on a stick that she used in darning.

Gramby always seemed to be busy doing something. When she was listening to the radio she had a needle in her hand, mending something, knitting, or sewing on a quilt. One evening she was working on a piece of cloth in a hoop using colored threads.

"What do you call that?"

"Embroidery. I get patterns at the sewing shop that I can iron on cloth and then stitch with these colored threads to make something pretty."

"That looks easy. Can I try it? Maybe I could make one of those dish-towels for Mama for her birthday."

"Of course."

And so I began a summer long effort to embroider a dishtowel to give Mama. I only worked at it on rainy days as I didn't want to miss base-ball or roaming the woods and creek. One rainy day I was concentrating hard on completing the dishtowel. I put the hoop on my leg for support to do some fine work, but when I lifted the hoop, I discovered that I had sewn a good portion of that particular area into my dungarees. I had to rip it out…with those tiny scissors…and redo that part of the design. I was pretty proud of the finished product. Gramby said I had done a marvelous job for my first project.

Mama kept that dishtowel hanging in her kitchen as long as she lived.

When I joined the Navy, Gramby sent me a sewing kit. It was a little larger than a deck of cards, complete with two needles of different size, black, white and khaki thread and buttons, a tiny pair of sharp pointed scissors…and a thimble.

Every kid should have a Gramby like that.

34

Thomas Rylee

Thomas "Big Tom" Rylee worked as an auto mechanic at Mr. Baggerly's Ford dealership. Baggersly's was the only automobile dealership in Coldbrook where you could purchase a new car. For anything new other than a Ford, you had to go to one of the larger towns nearby. It meant there were a lot of Fords in Coldbrook, so there was plenty of work for a good mechanic. Gramby said Big Tom was a fine one.

He was the father of my baseball buddy Tommy. Tommy asked me over to his house to see a scooter his Dad constructed using half of a pair of roller skates.

This was before skates came with the wheels built into the shoes. Roller skates then were adjustable metal contraptions that fit on your shoes. Each pair came with a skate key used to adjust the skate to the right length and width of the shoe. Skate keys were valuable pieces of equipment.

The problem with those skates was that all too often one skate would be damaged beyond repair, most frequently by knocking off a wheel and bending the frame on a crack in the pavement. The question then became what to do with the good half of the pair. Big Tom had an answer.

His Dad took the good skate apart and nailed the front and back parts to a short 2 by 4. Then he nailed on a wooden fruit box he got from Mr. Toler's New Food Emporium and attached a length of a broomstick across the top as a handle. Tommy had a workable scooter, that is until he hit the next crack in the pavement. He let me try it, and I said I would like to build one. I had an "orphan" skate I could use. He said he would help.

The day I went to his house, Tommy told me his Dad and his band were practicing in the garage. "Do you want to listen in?"

"Sure. What kind of a band is it?"

"Just come and listen."

There was a large group of people in the garage behind the house. Big Tom played a mandolin, and he introduced me to the rest. I recognized most of them from my trips around town. Ben Cooley, who worked at Fielder's Men's Store, played guitar; Joe Samuels from the Texaco station played bass; plumber Otis Brown played the banjo; and Mr. McKee who worked at the Ashley Funeral Home played fiddle. Tommy's mother sang and played harmonica, and his Aunt Nell sang and played a tambourine.

Tommy told me they played all over the county at different churches. "They write most of their own music but play a lot of songs that everyone knows."

It was the first time I heard Blue Grass Gospel. I loved it. I marveled at how fast they could move their fingers picking the instruments. I liked the harmony Tommy's mother and aunt sang. Each instrument would take a solo, backed by the others, and then they all came together for a big finale. They were having a fun time playing and singing together.

This introduction to Blue Grass music made me a fan for life. I stay on the alert to learn about Blue Grass Festivals nearby and try to support them when I can.

Big Tom's band played *Down by the Riverside*, a song I learned from Oholibama when I was at Uncle Zeet's handin' leaves. I started to sing along with them, and they smiled, kept playing, and nodded for me to keep singing. "Maybe we should let you join the group," Tommy's Mom said.

I listened until it was time to ride home for supper. I told Gramby about the music and how much I liked it. I said the group was playing at a country church west of Coldbrook the following Saturday evening.

"Do you think we could go? I would love to hear them play again. You would really like it."

"I think that would be a great idea. Why don't we do it."

Every kid should have a Gramby like that.

35

Lane Loudermilk Payne

Tweenlights on the porch were always good times to ask questions about this family's history.

"How did you meet Granddaddy Payne and get married?"

"I think I am the luckiest person in the world to have met and married Lane Loudermilk Payne."

"But how did you meet him? You weren't from Coldbrook. I'll bet there were plenty of young men near you trying to get you to marry them?"

"Not many. We lived in the country, and there were few so-called eligible bachelors roaming about. I did have two step cousins who were after me, but I wanted nothing to do with them. My Uncle Billy Hester was an old man when he married a widow woman, Aunt Mabel Skyler, who had twin sons just a few years older than I. Uncle Billy thought one of them would make a fine husband for me, but I…and my Papa…had other ideas. They lived on a farm near ours. The Skylar twins were lazy, ugly, and mean, and smelled of month old sweat, tobacco, moonshine whiskey, and cow manure. They spent their lives getting into trouble and out of work. When I was about fifteen, they cornered me and Bell in our barn with evil in their eyes. I brought Rufus to his knees with a kick to the groin, and Bell broke the nose of Felix with the dipper. They didn't bother us much after that. I would have gladly died than face the rest of my life with one of those apes."

"What ever happened to them?"

"Rufus died in a bawdy house fire up in Richmond, and Felix, who joined the Army, was hanged; he murdered his drill sergeant. A sad end to two no good scoundrels."

"So how did you get to Coldbrook?"

"I grew up on a farm, and, when I finished school, Papa said he wanted me to go to college. No women in my family had ever gone to college although most down through the generations went to local schools. My great, great Aunt Meredith Hester even wrote a book on etiquette; it was popular in the South before the Civil War. I was sixteen when I finished the county school. It was a big step when my Papa arranged for me to go to college at the Baptist School for Young Women in Lynchburg."

"That's a long way from where you grew up. Why did he pick that school?"

"He knew the head of the college. They were boyhood friends, and he became a Baptist minister. Papa had confidence it was a good place for me and that Reverend Browning would take good care of me. And he was right."

"I wanted to be a teacher, and after two years in Lynchburg I earned my certificate. They offered me a job to teach the third grade here in Coldbrook. I think what made the difference in my decision to come here was that Eloise Patterson was in my class. She was offered a job here to teach first grade. You know Miss Pat from the Library."

"Wow. You've known her that long?"

"Yes, we came here together and are still best friends. She taught for a few years, and then they asked her to take over the library. She's been there ever since. We roomed together at Thompson's boarding house uptown. Mrs. Thompson's daughter still runs it."

"Was Granddaddy living here then?"

"Yes. He was a very successful business man. He ran a farm supply store and was one of the leaders of the town. Everyone in town always called him by his full name…Lane Loudermilk Payne…and they did until the day he died."

"How did you meet him?"

"The first Sunday we were here, Miss Pat and I went to services at Coldbrook Baptist. Your grandfather was an usher that day, and he greeted us warmly and welcomed us to Coldbrook and to the church. He obviously knew we were the two new school teachers in town. It amazed me when a few weeks later he asked if I would do him the honor of allowing him to call on me at Mrs. Thompson's. This was Lane Loudermilk Payne, successful businessman, town leader, confirmed bachelor, and twice…*twice*…my age.

"How long before you got married?"

"He courted me for almost a year, until I had finished my year of teaching here in Coldbrook. I went home, but he came to see me most every Sunday. Your grandfather owned the first automobile in the county, and he drove it over awful roads…not really roads at all…to see me at home or at church. I was the envy of my cousins and neighbors. It was the first time many saw an automobile. Papa was not happy some old man was courting his young daughter, but he eventually accepted him and they became good friends. Sitting on this porch, he told me funny stories about those trips: getting stuck in mud holes and being pulled out by a team of horses, scaring people and animals, drawing so much curious attention from young boys."

"I wish I could have known him."

"I wish you could have too. He was a wonderful man, the most generous person I've ever known. He was a man of integrity, and everyone in Coldbrook trusted him. He had a reputation for standing by his word. He was generous with his money; he helped many people in this town when they were in need, and he tithed to the church his entire life.

"What is a tithe?"

"It's giving a tenth of your income to the work of the church. It was very important to him. He was also generous with his time; he was always available to help people whether or not they were business customers. He made it a priority to spend time with me and our children. You two could have had fun together. I can see you like many of the same things he did. He loved baseball and reading. He didn't go to college, but he read so much that everyone considered him one of the best educated men in Coldbrook."

"Baseball? Did he really like baseball?"

"Yes. He liked it so much that we got Aunt Bell to watch the children, and he took me on the train to Washington, D.C. to see the final game of the 1924 World Series. I don't know how he got those tickets. He said he wanted to show me off to those big city folks."

"Who won?"

"The Senators beat the New York Giants in the seventh game to win the Series. It was one of the most exciting times of my life…riding the train for the first time, going to Washington and back, staying in a big hotel, eating in fancy restaurants, seeing the monuments, and the Mall, and the Capitol, and the White House. It was wonderful being in the big crowd at the ball game and seeing the breathtaking finish when the home team won. I was a little country girl, and that was my first trip to a big city. I had no idea what it would be like."

"I hope I can see the World Series some time."

"Well, maybe…if the Senators ever get back in the Series…you can go."

"That doesn't look like it will happen soon."

"If your grandfather were here, I bet he would like talking with you about baseball."

"And I bet he liked bacon too."

"Indeed he did."

"We were married in my old home church, and there were a lot of Hesters there. My three sisters were bridesmaids. They were so excited to be part of a wedding and get dressed up and walk down the aisle with pretty bouquets of flowers. My mother made my dress from the one she wore when she married Papa."

"Until our marriage, he called me 'Miss Hester' and I spoke to him as 'Mr. Payne.' After the wedding and the celebration dinner, he carried me off in his car, and we went to the Burton Hotel in Danville for our first night together."

"When we were alone in our room, I said to him, 'Mr. Payne, I am so proud and happy to be your wife.' He kissed me for the first time. We lived here for over thirty wonderful years together before he died, and I never once called him anything other than 'Mr. Payne' for his entire life."

"What did he call you?"

"Sweetheart."

36

Gramby's Words to Live By

The four most important things you can say in your life:

I love you

I'm sorry

I forgive you

Thank you

In *this* family a gentleman always carries three handkerchiefs: one for show, one for blow, and one to offer a lady.

Do better today than you did yesterday.

Kill 'em with kindness. If you return bad for bad, you will keep an enemy. If you return good for bad, you just might gain a friend.

Be careful making promises. Be sure to keep them.

You learn a whole lot more listening than you do talking.

What *kind* of person do you want to be?

Always wear clean underwear. If you are in an accident, you don't want them to think you were raised poorly.

Fidelity, Integrity, and Generosity.

It's the butter on the corn.

In *this* family we hug.

Good intentions don't get the job done.

Read the Bible every day

Chase the Devil far away

Why don't we have some bacon!

37

Elizabeth Springer Hester Payne
1890-1986

Gramby died at home in Coldbrook after a brief illness, just a month shy of her ninety-sixth birthday. She left behind four children, eight grandchildren and seven great grandchildren. She left a legacy of family traditions, life-affirming wisdom, and love. It was the saddest day of my life when I got the phone call.

The funeral and related events lasted a good Coldbrook three days.

I was the first of her eight grandchildren to spend the summer with Gramby. Everyone thought the experience was so good for me that the rest of the grandkids were sent off in turn for a summer in Coldbrook. "Just look what it did for Charlie," they said

It should not be surprising that the eight of us are alike in so many ways.

We know how to iron, sew on a button, and talk on our hands.

We sing Gramby's songs when we get together, send post card thank-you's, have a library card, and buy heirloom tomatoes at the Farmers' Markets.

We love tweenlight, the smell of rain on dust, and the radio.

We hate ticks and chiggers and love trees and birds and butterflies.

We have taught our kids the knife and fork ritual and how to set the table the way we do it in *this* family.

We fix black-eyed peas, buttermilk biscuits, mashed potatoes, and brown sugar pie for special occasions.

We love to reminisce and talk about Aunt Bell, Doc GRAY-vuh-lee, Miss Pat, Mr. Willard, Naomi Parish, and Judge Law.

We boys have a Hargrove haircut.

We play cut-throat gin rummy with each other

How many times have our children heard us start a sentence with "In *this* family…," or "Why don't we…!"

We keep bacon grease in a pot on the stove.

They told me that when she died Gramby was wearing a pair of slacks. They were canary yellow.

She was a potato hole Hester.

After my summer in Coldbrook Gramby sent me a box of blackstrap cookies for Christmas…*every* Christmas.

Every kid should have a Gramby like that.

Glory Hallelujah!